SNIPER RIDGE

DAVID HEALEY

SNIPER RIDGE

By David Healey

Intracoastal Media digital edition published August 2020.

This book is a work of fiction. Names, characters, places and incidents are products of
the author's imagination or are used fictitiously. Any resemblance to actual events or
locales or persons, living or dead, is entirely coincidental.

Cover image by Streetlight Graphics.

BISAC Subject Headings:

FIC014000 FICTION/Historical

FIC032000 FICTION/War & Military

Only the dead have seen the end of war.

— PLATO

CHAPTER ONE

CAJE COLE HEARD a distant rifle shot and thought, *trouble*.

The thing about trouble was that it always seemed to find him. He couldn't avoid it. Here in Korea, trouble was about as hard to lose as his shadow.

Cole froze, listening for more gunfire, cocking his head toward the faint echo. His gray eyes were so clear that they looked out at the world with the ghostly gaze of Civil War soldiers in old photographs. His eyes also glittered with something like excitement now. He sniffed at the air. Deep down inside him, some part of Cole actually welcomed the trouble to come.

"Spread out," he warned the others. He was with a squad of a dozen soldiers. They were all good men, and he knew that he could trust them not to get each other killed out of sheer stupidity. However, exhaustion from humping up the steep hill had dulled their edge.

"C'mon, that's a long ways off," someone grumbled.

"If you can hear them shooting, then it ain't far enough," Cole snapped. He didn't bother to explain that the same rules applied to both gunshots and thunder. If you were close enough to hear either one, then you were close enough to be struck by a chunk of lead or a million volts of electricity—both of which had about the same result.

Cole was nominally in charge of this squad, which had been sent out to reconnoiter the hills beyond the U.S. and U.N. position near Triangle Hill. One thing about their platoon leader, Lieutenant Ballard, was that he was big on reconnoitering. Cole supposed they were lucky that the lieutenant hadn't decided to lead the squad himself. If that had happened, there was a good chance that none of them would have been coming back. The lieutenant probably had more pressing business, anyhow, like having to shine his butter bars.

Reconnoiter. That there was a fifty-cent word if he'd ever heard one.

Cole muttered, "Dang officers."

"What are you going on about?" the soldier to his left wanted to know. It was Pomeroy, another WWII veteran who'd had the bad luck, along with Cole, to find himself caught up in this Korean mess. Whereas Cole was lean and knotty like a locust fence post, Pomeroy was chunky with weight he'd put on after the last war and hadn't managed to lose in this one. Considering the lousy food and the constant exercise, that was something of an accomplishment. Pomeroy was breathing hard from the climb up the steep trail. Cole got a whiff of Pomeroy's fresh sweat and wished he hadn't. To be fair, didn't none of them smell too good. He took a couple of quick steps to stay upwind.

Pomeroy was also a veteran of the disaster that had been the retreat through the frozen landscape surrounding the Chosin Reservoir. Pomeroy had lost a couple of toes to frostbite for his trouble, but like an idiot, he had gotten himself sent back to Korea, when he should have been on his way back to the States. Cole shook his head, just thinking about that.

Off to his right walked Tommy Wilson, who had also been at the "Frozen Chosin" but who had managed to keep all of his toes, if not his innocence. Baby-faced and boyish, the kid looked a lot younger than he was. Cole recalled how he had seen this kid scream like a banshee as he plunged his bayonet into the belly of an enemy soldier. Still a teenager, the kid was definitely growing up fast here in Korea.

As much as he did, in fact, enjoy the company of Pomeroy and the kid, Cole would have preferred to be alone. But in the United States Army, there was no such thing, even when reconnoitering.

They moved higher onto the hill, onto open ground that was too rocky to grow much more than brambles and scrub trees. *Scald* was the word for this kind of barren landscape back home in the mountains.

Cole cast a nervous glance at the sky. The Corsair pilots tended to drop bombs and napalm—flaming jellied gasoline—on anything that moved in these mountains. From the air, it would be hard to tell them apart from a Chinese or North Korean patrol. So far, the drab sky appeared empty.

"What are you thinking?" Pomeroy asked quietly, which for him, sounded nearly like a shout. Pomeroy was a regular bull in a china shop most days. He was also going deaf from being too close to things that went *bang*. But the landscape and stillness at the top of the hill compelled them all to silence, as if they were in a church. Even the birds had fallen quiet.

"The lieutenant told us to take a look-see, so I reckon that's what we'll do."

"We could go back and tell him that we didn't see nothin'," Pomeroy said. He hawked and spat something thick and phlegmy into the dirt. "Wouldn't be a lie."

"Let's see if we can figure out who is doing that shooting."

"Screw the lieutenant," Pomeroy said. "Let's head back. We're pushing our luck as it is. You know as well as I do that if we run into anything bigger than a dishwashing detail, we're toast out here on our own."

"Don't get your knickers in a twist just yet."

"It's gonna be dark in a couple of hours," Pomeroy persisted.

Cole looked around at the squad. He could see from their faces that they were probably thinking much the same thing as Pomeroy. They'd be glad to return to the relative safety of the American lines. He saw faces pale with tiredness under the grime and stubble. "Let me just go on up here and take a look. Then we'll head back. Kid, you come with me."

Cole started forward, moving toward a higher point in the scree, from where he hoped to get a view of the next valley below. If he didn't see anything, they would turn around and head back. Even Cole didn't want to be caught out here after dark.

Not for the first time, Cole considered what a strange war this was in Korea. He almost missed World War II, just thinking about the difference. In Europe, the objective had been rather simple: land on the beach and push across Europe, all the way to Berlin. With a few exceptions, such as the Battle of the Bulge in the snowy Ardennes Forest, the American and Allied troops had mostly pushed forward as the Germans steadily retreated. Of course, the Germans had not given up easily ... in June 1944 in particular, it had seemed as if each acre of ground was hard won and soaked in blood.

Here in Korea, the war was more like some deadly football game. Both sides pressed back and forth, sometimes taking ground and sometimes losing it. Instead of yardage, they mostly fought over possession of these godforsaken hills and valleys. It was hard for an average soldier to define the objective, whereas in the last war, everyone in uniform knew that the goal was to march into Berlin or Tokyo.

Reaching the high point, Cole could see for miles. But it wasn't the distant mountains that caught his attention. In the valley below him, he could see a good-sized Chinese patrol about to attack a much smaller American squad. Like Cole's own group, they had likely been sent out to reconnoiter, but had gotten more than they bargained for.

That explained the rifle shot that they had heard earlier. Now, there were more and more shots. The distinctive cracks of rifle fire carried clearly on the clear air.

He and the kid had both crawled out onto the flat slab of rock, keeping as low as possible. No point in becoming a target for any pilots or sharp-eyed enemy soldiers. There were more than the soldiers in the valley to worry about. It was likely that a few pieces of Chinese artillery were hidden in the hills. Those big gunners had itchy trigger fingers.

"Look at that," said the kid, practically into Cole's ear. "It's like we have the bleacher seats at a football game ... one that's a long ways off."

"Ain't no game," said Cole, who had never sat in the bleachers or been to more than a pick-up football game—neither of those things existed back home in Gashey's Creek. "Our boys are about to get wiped out."

"Can't we do anything?" the kid asked. "We can go down there and help them out."

Cole shook his head. "Look at this ground. Steep and rocky. It would take us too long to get down there. Even then, there are an awful lot of the enemy and not enough of us."

"We've got to do something," the kid said urgently as the rate of fire increased below. Already, a couple of the Americans were down. Someone ran out and started dragging them toward cover.

Cole grunted, considering their options. "They're about a quarter of a mile away."

The kid was quiet a moment, then said, "That's about four football fields."

"Yeah? I call it half a second."

"Huh?"

"That's about how long it will take my bullet to get there. If whatever I'm aimin' at moves before then, there's a good chance that I'll miss."

The kid was staring at him. "Nobody can shoot that far, can they?"

"We'll see," said Cole, who wasn't one for bragging.

"What do you want me to do?"

"Take those binoculars and call me any targets you see. Once I get on scope, it's a right narrow field of view. And keep your eyes peeled. Pomeroy and the others are right behind us, so they've got our back, but for all we know this hillside could be crawlin' with the enemy."

He made a few adjustments to the telescopic sight on his Springfield rifle. He had picked it up at the end of the bitter Chosin Reservoir retreat and held onto it ever since. So far, Lieutenant Ballard hadn't taken it away from him, although that remained to be seen. The Springfield was essentially the same rifle that Cole had used in the last war. He knew it well, just the way a man might know every curve on the body of an old lover.

He put the rifle across a rock that he had padded with a rag. It made a damn near perfect bench rest, solid as the hill itself. Cole got comfortable behind it, spreading out his feet, locking his elbows into the ground, pressing his belly into the rock.

He fit the stock into the pocket created by his shoulder, then welded his cheek to the stock. Instantly, he smelled gun oil, gunpowder, and finely machined steel—three of the best smells on earth, in Cole's humble opinion. He put his gray eye to the scope until the scene in the valley below sprang closer. He shut out everything else.

As Cole's breathing slower, nearly stopped, he touched the pad of his right index finger to the trigger.

"Kid?" he exhaled.

"Machine gunners are setting up," he said. "Once they open fire—"

"Where?"

The kid told him and Cole found the target, a crew of two men getting a Degtyaryov light machine gun set up on its tripod. The Degtyaryov was a cruel bastard, cheaply made by the Soviets, with a circular magazine, jammed full of rounds, that sat atop the barrel. That weapon alone would literally cut the American defenders to pieces. The enemy soldiers were setting up behind a rock that gave them plenty of cover. Cole could barely see their heads and shoulders. Wasn't much of a target.

The kid was watching through the binoculars. "Nobody can hit that," he said. "Maybe if we head down there and get closer—"

Cole's crosshairs touched the helmet of the soldier on the right, the sight picture unwavering, thanks to the solid rock on which the rifle rested. His finger took up the last fraction of tension on the trigger.

The rifle fired.

At Cole's shoulder, the kid made a sound of surprise, eyes still glued to the binoculars. "You did it! I don't believe it."

Cole ran the bolt and loaded another round. Visible through the scope, the second machine gunner seemed to have frozen, surprised that his partner was now dead on the ground. He must have wondered where the shot had come from. Cole didn't let him wonder for long.

At this range, the round was still traveling at nearly 2000 feet per second and hitting with 1400 foot-pounds of energy—more than half a ton of whomp ass.

When another two men moved to man the machine gun, Cole shot them, too.

Cole pulled himself away from the rifle long enough to look back and see Pomeroy approaching with the rest of the squad. They took up positions on the ridge and began to pour fire down at the enemy troops. It was a long way for them to shoot and hit anything, but he reckoned that even a blind squirrel finds a nut now and then.

"That officer there," the kid whispered, as if the Chinese soldiers far below could hear him. Cole himself could barely hear the kid over the ringing in his ears. After all, each detonation of a .30-06 round smacked his eardrum like a thunderclap. He was developing a permanent ringing. "He's organizing things."

"Got him," Cole said.

He could see that the officer was trying to set up an attack on the outnumbered Americans down there. The Chinese favored swarm tactics, throwing everything they had at a section of the enemy line in hopes of overwhelming it—never mind how many soldiers they themselves lost in the process. One thing about the Chinese and North Koreans was that they never thought twice about getting their own men killed.

Still, the enemy tactics were just a bit more complex. At the same time that the swarm attack was happening, a smaller force typically tried to flank the defenders in the confusion and wreak havoc in the rear by attacking supply vehicles or even hospital tents. The little squad down below had neither, but that didn't mean some of the attackers wouldn't try to get in behind them.

Cole put his sights on the Chinese officer and fired. The man flung out his arms and died as dramatically as some two-bit actor in a war movie.

Barely pausing, Cole fired again and again. Now, instead of being pinned down, the squad below was on the attack, slamming into the now-disorganized Chinese ranks. The enemy began to scatter before the onslaught. Cole reloaded and fired, adding as much chaos as possible to the enemy's situation.

While the enemy troops below hadn't figured out the location of the sniper, someone else had. A couple of bright flashes appeared on the gloomy hillside in the distance, followed by the telltale whistle of artillery shells. The Chinese gunners hidden in the hills must have spotted Cole and his squad on the ridge.

"Cole!" the kid shouted. "Time to go!"

The kid started to get up, but Cole reached up and yanked him off his feet just as the first shell hit a tree no more than a hundred feet away. Whirling fragments of metal and jagged splinters of pine filled the air like a sudden squall of rain. The second shell hit the hillside and showered them all with rock and dirt.

"Go!" Cole shouted, leaping up and screaming at the squad. Miraculously, none of them had been hit. They didn't need to be told twice, but scrambled off the crest of the ridge. Two more shells hit, just short of where the men had been positioned only moments ago. Before the Chinese battery could fire again, the squad was on the other side of the ridge, out of sight.

"All in a day's work," said Pomeroy, who was limping after the sprint off the hilltop. Most of the time he hid it, but it was clear that his feet still hurt him. "Guess we showed them."

Cole thought about the officer he had seen die through the rifle scope. In the last war, at first, he had kept count of how many enemy soldiers he had killed. Then, he had stopped. Enemy or not, a man's soul was not a trophy to be tallied.

"Let's move out," he said, raising his voice so that the whole squad could hear. He had a surprisingly high-pitched, twangy voice. It was easy to imagine him suddenly breaking into a Rebel Yell. "Go on now! We best get back before dark. Keep your distance and keep your eyes open—there's no telling how many other Chinese squads might be out here. I hope to hell that we ain't gone and woke up the dragon."

Leading the way, rifle at the ready, he moved silently into the dense scrub trees and seemed to disappear into the gray underbrush.

CHAPTER TWO

FROM THE PASSENGER seat of the speeding Jeep, Don Hardy observed that the landscape was unlike anything he had seen before. He was a little awed by it, in fact—the jagged mountains against the distant icy blue sky, the dusty hills, Korean farmers working their fields using yoked pairs of oxen. *You're not in Kansas anymore*, he reminded himself.

Then again, Hardy wasn't actually from Kansas, but close enough. He was from Indiana, Hoosier country. He looked like he could have been a midwestern farm boy himself, big and rawboned, ruggedly handsome in a blue-eyed, sandy-haired way.

But Hardy sure wasn't a farmer. He wasn't a soldier, either. He was a journalist, with a newly minted degree from Purdue University. He had been able to finish his degree with a deferment, but the ink had hardly dried when the Army got its hands on him and he was on the way to Korea. It was a rude awakening, being yanked from civilian life into uniform—or as one of his college friends might have put it more crudely, it sure would have been nice to be kissed before he was screwed.

Hardy sat beside his driver in the Jeep bouncing its way along the rough road toward the Taebaek Mountains, away from the coastline where Hardy had landed just a few days ago. Being a budding wordsmith, he searched his mind for descriptive snippets from all of the Faulkner, Hemingway, and Wolfe that he had read as an English major. He would need to include some details in the news article that he would be writing for *Stars & Stripes*. It didn't occur to him yet that his audience would already be quite familiar with the landscape.

He took his helmet off, to better enjoy the fresh breeze, which was spoiled only by a slight scent of ... he wrinkled his nose, trying to pinpoint the odor.

"Best keep that on," the driver said. "Captain Dorchester will chew my ass if you get your head shot off before you get to take pictures of anything with that camera of yours."

"Has a helmet ever stopped a bullet?"

"Not that I've heard of, but there's always a first time."

Hardy put his helmet back on, just in case. Captain Dorchester was the editor of *Stars & Stripes*, and he didn't want to cross him, dead or not. Dorchester was a pudgy little ogre of a man who showed next to no patience with the fresh-faced reporters and photographers that he was sending out to document the war. Like some caricature of a big city editor, he kept a cigar clamped between his yellowed teeth and a bottle of scotch hidden in his desk drawer.

The publication itself was supposed to be quasi-military and independent, and yet the newspaper's staff followed a military hierarchy, with most of the editors being officers and most of the reporters and photographers being newly minted privates like Hardy. There wasn't any saluting, but there was a definite pecking order. Still, Hardy supposed it might land him a newspaper job back home. Not only that, but it sure as hell beat being an infantryman in a foxhole.

Hardy wrinkled his nose again. "What *is* that smell?" he wanted to know.

The driver barked a laugh. "What's the matter, haven't you ever smelled an outhouse before? This whole place is one big latrine. That's because all the farmers fertilize their fields with, you know, shit."

Hardy realized that he had a lot to learn about Korea.

Guys who had been there a while might have said, *Good luck with that, buddy.*

Testing out his journalistic skills, Hardy had already ventured to ask some of the soldiers that he'd met so far in Korea what the objective for the war was, and had mostly received blank stares. He turned to the driver.

"Hey, do you know what this war is all about? What we're fighting for, I mean?"

The driver barely gave him a horrified look. "What are you, one of those secret Communists they keep warning us about? Don't tell me I drove a Communist all the way out here."

"Oh, never mind," Hardy said, deciding that he had better keep his mouth shut unless he wanted to get out and walk. He went back to brooding over the landscape.

So much for that. Still, Hardy struggled to define the war clearly in his own mind.

The purpose of the war wasn't to defeat and invade China. Maybe it was to liberate North Korea. Or was the goal to make the Communists stay or their own side of the 38th parallel? The last two objectives might even have been obtainable if it hadn't been for a few hundred thousand screaming Chinese. In the end, the goal wasn't only uncertain, it was downright murky. And often, the goal changed from week to week. It was one hell of a slippery subject to write about, that was for damn sure.

Hardy had been sent by the irascible Captain Dorchester to document some of the fighting that was taking place in a new push to dislodge the enemy. He wasn't completely sure if the editor really wanted the latest news and some photographs, or if he was just trying to get Hardy out from underfoot. And if he didn't come back, to the editor's way of thinking, it might just be one less reporter to worry about.

"Find some happy news," Dorchester had ordered, although the captain didn't appear to be familiar with that particular emotion himself, poking the much-taller young reporter in the chest to emphasize his point. "These articles also get read by people back home. They need to hear about how their soldiers are fighting the good fight. They need some good news for a change, God knows."

It would be Hardy's job to interview some soldiers at the front, report on how the UN forces were winning Operation Showdown to drive the Chinese off these hills, and even to take a few pictures. He had been supplied with a small, state-of-the-art Kodak camera for this very purpose. The reporters at *Stars & Stripes* often had to do double-duty by taking photographs as well as writing articles.

Captain Dorchester had poked him in the chest one last time before he left and warned him, "If you break that goddamn camera, it's coming out of your pay. Understood?"

"Yes, sir."

He had then saluted Captain Dorchester, who rolled his eyes. The military press corps was not big on saluting. "Oh, for chrissakes. Get the hell out of here!"

So far, Hardy's only previous assignment had been to cover Marilyn Monroe's visit to the troops as part of a USO tour. He had been excited about seeing such a big star in person, and he wasn't disappointed. The military's own press corps always managed to be right up front when one of the big stars arrived on a USO tour, and Marilyn Monroe had been no exception.

Her visit was already well-covered by reporters and photographers, meaning that Hardy really didn't have a role to play in that regard, but a buddy had found Hardy a spot right up front, supposedly helping with the microphones and other equipment.

Wow, had she been a knockout. She wasn't much of a singer; it was more like she talked her way through "Diamonds Are A Girl's Best Friend" and other songs in a sultry bedroom voice, but most soldiers weren't interested in the quality of her singing. Heck, even her band had the suggestive name of *Anything Goes*.

You couldn't hear much of her singing, anyhow, on account of all the hooting, catcalls, and whistling. To his surprise, a group of black soldiers was in the front row, although their enthusiasm seemed subdued. Maybe they felt like they shouldn't show too much excitement over a white woman.

To be sure, that woman could fill out a dress. The fabric hugged her hips and thighs, and despite the chill, she showed off her shoulders and revealed plenty of cleavage.

Up on the rough stage, surrounded by drab tents and dull landscape, she had looked incredibly out of place, like a diamond in a sea of coal. The thought occurred to him that she must be kind of chilly up there. Back home, she could live at the Ritz and wear all the furs she wanted. But she didn't complain, and she put on one hell of a show for the boys. Hardy had come to the realization that the soldiers weren't the only heroes that day.

* * *

PREPARING for his first trip to the front, Hardy had looked through the clip files to get a sense of what *Stars & Stripes* wanted in its pages. Mostly, the reporting was heavy on interviewing soldiers about what they missed back home and short on any strategy details. There was lots of praise for their bravery and accounts of heroic actions. In his quest to figure out the war, the picture of the Korean conflict that Hardy had pieced together so far was not a great one.

First, the North Korean communist forces had initially swept through the entire peninsula with overwhelming success, capturing all of the major cities. The small American military presence had been unprepared to fend them off and had really been knocked back on its heels. The simple truth was that the peacetime military in the Pacific had gone soft and let its guard down.

Then, that old warhorse General Douglas MacArthur had roused himself long enough from his cushy headquarters in Japan to plan a daring but brilliant amphibious invasion at Inchon and consequent breakout from the Pusan Perimeter, where US and South Korean troops were hemmed in. The tables had soon turned, and it was the North Korean communist guerrillas who were in full retreat. But US and UN forces under MacArthur's right-hand man, General Almond, had overreached themselves, pushing relentlessly toward the Chinese border at the Yalu River.

Chairman Mao had not been eager to embrace the idea of a US-controlled territory on his borders, or with having troops from the world's democracies breathing down his neck. A hop, skip, and jump away, Uncle Joe Stalin had come to the same conclusion. The Soviets sent military advisors and supplies to the Chinese. Before long, Chairman Mao had unleashed masses of Chinese troops into the conflict, resulting in the disastrous Chosin Reservoir campaign for the Americans and UN. For days back home, newspaper headlines had trumpeted grim news about the war and the surrounded troops in every city and small town. The US troops had narrowly avoided complete annihilation.

Since then, there had been some changes in leadership. Part of the trouble with Korea was that there had not been a continuity in leadership, as there had been in Europe under General Eisenhower. General MacArthur had been replaced by General Ridgway who had been replaced by General Van Fleet, who was now in overall command. President Truman was still proving himself to be an ineffectual, hands-off leader who was content to rely on reporters filtered through the military than to see the situation for himself. He was definitely no FDR or Churchill.

The war continued to be limited, in that nuclear weapons were off the table. At the same time, Truman had opted against allowing the bombing of bases in China or any bridges across the Yalu River in an effort to avoid a larger conflict. The cost of that decision was that the Chinese forces in Korea could be resupplied with impunity. It was a bit like trying to use buckets to catch all the water coming out of a fire-hose, rather than turning off the valve.

Meanwhile, thousands of drafted American boys who didn't really want to be there had died, mostly fighting drafted Chinese boys. To use the term "boys" was not an exaggeration. Enlisted men in Korea were typically ages seventeen to twenty-four, although there were a few older Second World War veterans in the ranks. South Korean boys were drafted to fight starting at age sixteen. As usual, old men went to war and expected boys to do the actual fighting.

* * *

HARDY'S MUSINGS on the landscape and the war were interrupted by the driver.

"There it is," said the driver, taking his hands off the Jeep's bucking steering wheel long enough to point. "Triangle Hill. That's where we're headed."

The road wound its way across an open plain, but Hardy looked ahead at the mountains and hills they were driving toward. He saw one rounded peak that rose above the others. It wasn't clear to him how this was a military objective of obvious strategic value because it looked much like the hills surrounding it, just a little taller.

"Doesn't look like much to fight over."

The driver laughed. "You are a regular green bean, aren't you? If you do find anything in this place worth fighting over, that's going to be headline news, Mr. Reporter."

"If you say so," Hardy said, unable to keep an annoyed tone out of his voice. He didn't need a Jeep driver telling him what to write about.

But the driver just chuckled, apparently amused by his passenger's lack of knowledge. Helpfully, the driver pointed out the other nearby hills and peaks. "Now, just in front of Triangle Hill, that's what they call Pike's Peak. Off to the left is the hill called Jane Russell, on account of it looking like a pair of tits. To the right is Sniper Ridge. You can probably figure out why it's called that."

"What do the Chinese call these hills?"

The driver barked another laugh. "Buddy, they call them *theirs*."

That explanation sounded ominous to Hardy, who began to feel a soupçon of concern, like that first tickle you get in the back of the throat as the flu comes on.

Slowly, the mountains loomed closer with each passing mile. The rough road carried them into the US base camp. He saw sandbags stacked around machine gun emplacements and tangled rows of concertina wire gathered like prickly tumbleweeds. Some of the sandbags were leaking sand, and he realized that these were bullet holes.

A few men glanced with curiosity at the approaching Jeep, but Hardy's arrival didn't keep their attention for long when they realized that the Jeep held only a couple of soldiers and not the brass. Anymore, most of the high-ranking officers flew in by helicopter to avoid the danger of being ambushed on the road. The sight of one of these ungainly "choppers" remained a novelty. If you weren't a general, your only chance of getting a ride on one was if you were wounded and lucky enough to be flown out to one of the new MASH units. Nobody wanted that kind of luck.

These men looked like they had been through the wringer. Streaked with mud, their worn uniforms had seen better days. Helmets bore scratches and dents—even bullet holes. One helmet that he spotted had a Confederate flag painted on the front. The eyes under the helmet flicked at him and Hardy recoiled at the soldier's pale gray stare that seemed to instantly dismiss him, like a wolf looking for worthier prey. These were hard men at the front. Some of them had that unfocused gaze of men who had seen too much and looked through Hardy and the Jeep without seeing them at all.

The faces that weren't covered in several days of stubble looked haggard. Nobody seemed particularly friendly, and Hardy gulped, just thinking about trying to interview one of these hard cases—or God forbid, take their picture for *Stars & Stripes*.

"Here you go, delivered safe and sound at HQ, which is sayin' something these days," the driver announced, pulling to a stop in front of what could only be described as a sandbagged bunker. The driver made no move to switch off the engine or to help Hardy with his duffel bag. "Hurry up and get your gear unloaded. I want to get back before dark, or I probably *won't* make it back, if you know what I mean."

Hardy had barely pulled his gear off the rear seat before the Jeep was rolling away, back the way it had come. Watching it go, despite the excitement of being on his first real assignment on the front lines, he regretted that he wasn't going back with it.

He hefted his duffel bag to his shoulder and headed for HQ. The sentries didn't try to stop him, so he walked right in. The dark space reeked of burnt coffee and stale cigarette smoke. He checked in with a harried sergeant sitting at a typewriter and got sent from one desk to another until he found himself in the presence of a major named Severn.

"*Stars & Stripes*, huh?" the major said.

"Yes, sir. I'm reporting on conditions here at the front, how the men are doing."

"In that case, I hope you can write good fiction," the major said.

Hardy wasn't sure what to say to that. "I'll be taking photographs too, sir."

"Well, it's about time these boys got some attention," the major said. He put on a thinking face. "I'll assign you to Fox Company. That's Lieutenant Ballard. If there's one man in this Army who will love to see a reporter and get his picture taken, it's Ballard."

"Yes, sir."

"All right, son, now get out of here and try not to get yourself killed before you can make us famous."

Hardy saluted and turned to go, but the major called him back. "Hold on a minute, son." He looked Don up and down, as if noticing him critically for the first time. "Where is your weapon? Don't you have a rifle?"

"I wasn't issued one, sir. They gave me a camera instead. I'm a journalist."

"Try explaining that to the Chinese when they start shooting at you. What kind of idiot would send you into the field without a weapon?" The major sighed. "Listen, son, shooting pictures is fine, but be prepared to shoot a few bullets as well. On your way out, tell the sergeant there that you need to be issued a weapon."

"Yes, sir."

Hardy found the sergeant, a grizzled looking old campaigner, and was issued an M-1 carbine.

"Remember how to use this thing?" the sergeant asked.

"Sure," said Hardy, who hadn't touched a weapon since basic training. He didn't sound all that convincing.

"That's what I thought." The sergeant gave him a quick refresher, emphasizing that the safety should be left on at all times and that he had better be careful about where he pointed the muzzle, and then handed him two magazines. "Here's a bit of advice. Save your last bullet."

"Sir?"

"If the Chinese overrun your position, you'll want that last bullet for yourself. But don't put that in your article."

Wondering what he had gotten himself into, Hardy gulped and went to find Fox Company and Lieutenant Ballard.

CHAPTER THREE

COLE and the rest of the squad threw themselves down in exhaustion. They had trooped back into the base, worn out from the trek through the mountains. Adrenalin from the one-sided skirmish and bombardment left them feeling hollowed out and empty.

"I can't believe we made it back here in once piece," Pomeroy said. "I thought for sure that we'd be ambushed."

"I reckon we got lucky," Cole agreed. "Them Chinese hereabouts is thick as fleas on a coon hound."

"One thing about you, Hillbilly, is that you've got a way with words," Pomeroy said.

The trek back to the base had been harrowing, indeed. At any moment, they had expected to be attacked by superior numbers of Chinese soldiers. The hills swarmed with the enemy. They considered it a minor miracle that they had made it back.

Now, the soldiers sprawled on the ground in the way that only exhausted men can do, looking more like rag dolls than soldiers. Rumor had it that there might still be some chow at the mess tent, but that meant rising from the ground and walking that much farther. For men whose feet and legs already ached, it was too much to ask.

"To hell with it," said Pomeroy, casting a longing glance in the direction of the mess tent, then shaking his head. "Might as well be a hundred miles away, as far as I'm concern."

"Got that right," Cole agreed.

He opened some rations and wolfed down a meal, and the others who had enough energy for it followed suit.

"That was one hell of a lop-sided fight today," Pomeroy said. "We did some damage to those Chinese."

"I reckon we got lucky," Cole said. "Although I got to say, it's a good thing we got out of there in one piece. Another couple of minutes and that Chinese artillery would've turned us inside out."

Pomeroy nodded and lit a cigarette. He knew that Cole meant *literally* turned inside out—they had both seen what artillery could do to infantrymen. He offered a cigarette to Cole, who shook his head. Cole hadn't been smoking for a while now—not since returning from Europe, as a matter of fact—and was glad of it. He had a lot more wind when out on patrol than Pomeroy did, or even some of these youngsters just out of high school.

He mused that he had been leading a clean life back home in the mountains, staying away from tobacco and whiskey—it was just shooting people that he couldn't seem to avoid. Cole had come across two dirtballs who were about to assault a woman whose car had broken down. They had made the mistake of drawing on Cole when he had interfered with their plans. The judge and sheriff had come up with the solution that their local war hero could avoid jail by joining the Army. As a result, here he was in Korea, with a rifle in his hands.

Maybe there was something wrong with him because he didn't mind all that much.

Cole snorted at that thought.

"What?" Pomeroy wanted to know.

Cole just shook his head.

Instead of a smoke after his meal, which was something of a ritual for many men, Cole opted to clean his rifle. He removed the bolt and set it aside, then began wiping down the action and all the metal parts of his rifle in order to prevent any rust from the salt and oils of his hands. There was even a rumor that he had the cleanest rifle in the United States Army.

The Springfield was one tough customer, mostly reliable as an old boot and with roots as a military firearm that went clear back to the Great War, but that didn't stop Cole from babying his rifle. One thing for sure, that rifle had gotten a workout today and now had powder grime clogging its lands and grooves. Cole gently worked an oil-soaked rag deep into the action, almost lovingly. By now, his fingers recognized every divot in the wood grain, every scratch on the barrel. Back at the Chosin Reservoir, that extra oil had gummed up the actions of many rifles, but no one was predicting that it would.

Cole knew a rifle was just wood and metal and a handful of moving parts, but wasn't it something more than that? A rifle had personality. This one had sure as hell saved his life a few times. And taken a few lives, as well.

"Goddamn, Hillbilly, you could do surgery with his rifle," Pomeroy remarked.

"What the hell kind of surgery would you do with a rifle?" Cole wondered.

"I don't know—remove someone's heart, or maybe their liver."

"Well, I do reckon that's my kind of surgery." Cole looked over at Tommy Wilson, who had followed Cole's lead and was now busy cleaning his own rifle. "You done good today, kid."

"Yeah? I guess I'm starting to get the hang of this soldiering thing," the kid said.

"Don't get too good at it, or you'll end up like us," Cole said. "Stuck in the Army."

"Practice makes perfect," Pomeroy added. "The good news is that you can wake up tomorrow morning and practice all over again."

Cole added with a grin, "And if you mess up while you're practicing, the worst that can happen is that you'll end up dead."

"You two really know how to cheer a guy up," the kid said. "Gee, thanks."

All around them, the camp was busy getting ready for nightfall. For the most part, the daylight hours meant that the US defenses were fairly protected thanks to the air cover and the artillery that could target any troop movements in the hills. However, by night, all bets were off because the enemy could move unseen. Most of the attacks by the Chinese and North Korean forces took place under cover of darkness.

The encampment was far enough from the enemy positions to avoid drawing sniper fire, so some of the squads had small fires that they used to heat up their rations or to make hot water for coffee. They could smell some of those delicious smells now. Cole's squad was too damn tired to make any effort to build a fire.

The air had an autumn chill to it, but was pleasant enough with the tang of woodsmoke from the fires. It all could have been like a camping trip if the enemy hadn't been out there. Every now and then, a Jeep roared in and another Jeep roared out, carrying what they thought must have been urgent messages. Cole figured that at least it gave the officers something to do, so that they left everybody else alone.

They were all still sitting there when one of Cole's least favorite officers came walking up to them. It was Lieutenant Ballard.

For whatever reason, Ballard had taken a dislike to Cole. Cole had to admit that the feeling was mutual. There was maybe something classist to it. Ballard was tall and well-built, handsome even, and a college graduate. He looked down his long nose at dirt-poor soldiers like Cole.

The lieutenant was not alone, but had a small retinue with him. He was trailed by Sergeant Weber, another survivor of the Chosin Reservoir fight. Tough and capable, Weber was also a veteran of the Wehrmacht. Like Weber, a number of former German soldiers had found themselves wearing US uniforms. Soldiering was the only career that old Weber knew. He and Cole had formed a mutual respect, if not quite a bond. After all, it was the lieutenant who buttered Weber's bread, not Cole.

Cole took stock of the other soldiers. He recognized most of them, but one new face caught Cole's eye. This soldier carried himself like a veteran of more than one fight, signaled by his sturdy build and helmet set at a cocky angle. However, he was only an enlisted man. What did Ballard want with him?

The other soldier in the group still wore a relatively new and clean uniform, which marked him as being new to Triangle Hill. He was tall and raw-boned, like he was no stranger to hard physical work, but he lacked the economical movements of men who had crossed miles and miles of Korea. Improbably, he carried a camera on a strap around his neck and a small notebook dwarfed by his big hand. A carbine was slung across his shoulder like an after-thought.

Curiously, this soldier seemed busy writing down everything that Ballard said. It wouldn't have been all that unusual to see someone like General MacArthur have someone hang on his every word, but not Ballard. He kept glancing at the reporter, as if to make sure that he hadn't missed anything.

Whatever was going on, they were about to find out.

"I've been waiting for you to get back," Ballard said, stopping in front of Cole, who raised himself wearily to his feet. Other officers would have told him to stay put, but not Ballard. "Where the hell have you been?"

"We ran into some trouble, sir."

"You were on a simple recon mission."

Quickly, Cole explained about coming across the unit that had needed some help against the Chinese, but Ballard didn't look convinced.

"I didn't send you out there to play cavalry," he said. "I sent you out there to gather intelligence. We need information, dammit."

"Well, sir, we learned that there is a squad of Chinese soldiers down in the Valley and that there is artillery within range up on Jane Russell," Cole said. "How's that for information?"

Cole knew that his tone was walking the line in terms of insubordination, but he didn't much care.

Ballard was glaring at him. Over the lieutenant's shoulder, the sergeant gave him a barely perceptible shake of the head. Warning him.

For all that Cole knew, he had fought against Sergeant Weber in the last war, but the sergeant was all right. He was gruff and a stickler for the rules, which you might expect from a German, but he was fair enough. Right now, he was trying to save Cole's bacon.

Cole and Weber had gotten off on the wrong foot after Cole's initial arrival in Korea. Weber had thought that Cole was too lazy or too scared to fight. He couldn't have been more wrong about that.

Their ordeal at the Chosin Reservoir had helped them gain a grudging respect for one another.

Ballard, on the other hand, had also been at the "Frozen Chosin," but seemed to ignore the experience like one might ignore a bad dream.

Cole couldn't blame him because it wasn't something that anyone wanted to remember. Maybe Ballard thought that being part of that disastrous withdrawal was a black mark against his record. Although the soldiers in the field didn't have much access to newspapers or radio news, rumors had been going around that there was a lot of fallout from the Chosin Reservoir campaign. Back home, some called it a cowardly retreat and a defeat.

What the hell did they know about it? Cole wondered. Those who said that the Chosin was a defeat hadn't been there when thousands of screaming enemy troops swarmed at them out of the darkness. They hadn't been there when it got so cold that the rifle actions froze up and some men died of exposure overnight in their foxholes. They hadn't been there when the truckloads of wounded had to be abandoned so that their fellow soldiers were bayoneted shot and burned alive by the Chinese.

Cole tugged his thoughts back to the present. Keeping the sergeant's warning glance in mind, Cole finally responded with a simple, "Yes, sir."

Ballard glared at him for another long moment, then raised his voice to address the entire squad. He half-turned toward the other men accompanying him, so that they would be included in his comments. "Listen up, everyone. We've been chosen to have a reporter from *Stars & Stripes* tag along with us for a few days. Private Hardy will be taking a few pictures and talking to you. I expect that you will give him your full cooperation."

"Talk to a reporter? Not me," Cole muttered. He'd had that experience in the last war, when none other than the famous war correspondent Ernie Pyle had interviewed him. In Cole's estimation, the story had only brought him a lot of trouble.

"What's that, Cole?" Ballard snapped.

"Nothing, sir."

Ballard went on. "I expect you to give Private Hardy your full cooperation," he said. "The folks back home need to know what sort of job
we're doing."

"Yes, sir."

But the lieutenant wasn't done. "Now that we have a reporter with
us, I wanted to make sure that he had something to report," Ballard
said. He turned to indicate the other man accompanying him, who had
been standing there like a tree stump. "I want you to meet Heywood.
He's a sniper, one of the first from the new U.S. Army training school.
I had to pull some strings to get him assigned to our platoon. It's going
to make a great newspaper story. He's here to teach you boys a thing or
two about sniper tactics and hitting a target at any kind of distance."

The kid spoke up, "Sir, you should have seen Cole today—"

Ballard waved a hand to cut him off. "That's exactly what I'm
talking about. No more cowboy stuff. We need some real training
around here, which is why I've brought in Heywood. However, I've got
to say that there is a shortage of sniper rifles." He glanced at the
reporter. "Don't put that in the article. Anyhow, we've got a surplus of
snipers and a shortage of sniper rifles."

"That's the Army for you," Pomeroy said.

The lieutenant pointed at Cole's Springfield rifle, which was still
disassembled nearby. "That's what I'm talking about right there, a
sniper rifle. We need to put sniper rifles in the hands of actual Army-
designated snipers. Cole, reassemble that rifle and hand it over to
Heywood."

"Sir?" Cole didn't make any move to obey the lieutenant's orders.

"You heard me. Hurry it up, Cole. I haven't got all day. We'll get
you a carbine instead."

Nearby, the men of the squad seem to hold their collective breath.
They knew very well what Cole could do with a rifle. They had seen
him in action again and again. Just today, he had decimated an enemy
unit at long range.

Now, here was Ballard wanting to take away Cole's rifle. What the
hell was he thinking? It sounded as if he just wanted to make himself
look good for the press. Knowing Ballard, he couldn't make captain
soon enough.

Of course, none of them said a word out loud to the lieutenant. As for Cole, he stared at Ballard just long enough with his flat gray eyes that the lieutenant was forced to look away.

"You heard me, Cole," the lieutenant said. "That's a direct order. Give that rifle to Heywood. Right now, son! Give him whatever else he needs, too. I'm going to take Private Hardy over here to interview some of the other men for *Stars & Stripes*, and when I come back, I want this transfer to be done."

Lieutenant Ballard walked off with the reporter in tow.

Cole didn't respond at first, seeming to be thinking it over, as if he had some choice other than following orders. "Aw, to hell with it," he finally said, then reached over and reassembled the rifle, finally sliding the bolt into place and offering the weapon to Heywood.

Their new designated sniper was about five-foot-ten and solidly built, maybe a bit shorter than Cole by an inch or two, but far heavier. He looked like he could be a bruiser when he needed to be.

He accepted the rifle without a word of thanks, and his broad face held a challenge.

"So you're Cole," he said. "I think I've heard about you."

Pomeroy spoke up. "You probably *did* hear about him, buddy. Cole here has those Chinese bastards afraid of him, and for good reason."

"Is that right?" Heywood smirked. "What I heard was that you had lost your nerve. That's why the unit needs a good sniper."

"I don't know where you heard that," Cole said, truly surprised. "Who said that I've lost my nerve?"

"Heywood here needs to check his sources," Pomeroy said. "He got some bad information. For example, who said that he was a good sniper?"

Heywood glared at Pomeroy, and then turned his attention back to Cole. "The lieutenant told me that," Heywood said.

"You mean Ballard says I've lost my nerve?" Cole supposed that he shouldn't be surprised, considering that the lieutenant had it in for him. "That sneaky no good snake-eyed son of a—"

"Uh, Cole," Pomeroy growled a warning. "You might want to hold that thought. Here he comes."

At that moment, Lieutenant Ballard came walking over, having left the reporter to gather the other men's names and stories. *Swaggering* over, was more like it, Cole thought.

Heywood moved to take the rifle out of Cole's hands.

Cole didn't let go right away. Heywood was wide and sturdy, but he looked surprised by the iron grip that he encountered. He pulled harder.

The tug of war went on for several seconds as Ballard approached. When Cole did suddenly let go, Heywood had to dance back on his heels, having been thrown off balance.

As for Cole, he instantly felt like a lion that had just lost its mane. Thunder without its clap.

He kept seeming to lose things in this war. A Chinese soldier had taken his Bowie knife off him when he'd briefly been a prisoner of war back at the Chosin Reservoir. *The goddamn enemy stole my knife. And now this human stump has got my rifle.*

It wasn't the first time that he had been ordered to relinquish a rifle. However, the circumstances had definitely been different. The last time, in the last war, a vainglorious officer had foolishly wanted Cole's rifle for himself. Cole hadn't been left with any choice. That officer hadn't lasted more than a day as a sniper—and Cole hadn't even been the one to kill him.

This time was somewhat different. What the lieutenant wanted was to get his name in the newspaper and advance his military career by advancing the new sniper program.

Poor ol' Heywood didn't know what he was in for. He was about to become the lieutenant's whipping boy. Cole almost felt sorry for him.

Almost.

"Make sure you keep her oiled up," Cole said. "I don't want my rifle all rusty when I get her back."

Heywood stared at him, puzzled.

The lieutenant walked up.

"All right then," Ballard said. "You men get a good night's sleep. You'll be going out on patrol again first thing in the morning.

"Yes, sir," said Cole, who had been the squad leader.

"Oh, but not you, Cole," Ballard said. "Pomeroy here will be in charge of the squad. You can head on over to the mess tent. In fact, I think they could use some help there right now."

"Yes, sir," Cole said flatly.

"You see, we've got our designated sniper now. The kitchen could use some help. I know you were good at that before. I seem to recall you started out in the mess tent when you got to Korea last fall. It's important to get some hot meals to the men so that they don't have to eat rations all the time."

"Yes, sir," Cole said. "I reckon I'll be reporting to the mess tent."

CHAPTER FOUR

HAVING DODGED YET another aerial attack, the vehicle carrying Chen Li raced down the mountain road. Chen hung on for dear life as the Soviet-made GAZ-67—the Communist answer to the American Jeep— followed the curving road, veering perilously close to the edge. The road had been cut into the face of the mountain, and beyond the edge was a steep fall to the valley floor, several hundred feet below. Chen looked out into the thin air and felt dizzy.

There were no guard rails, and it was a long way down. Chen knew because he had made the mistake of leaning out to take a look. The view of the valley below left his stomach churning. Needless to say, he wouldn't be doing that again.

Even to call this a road was something of an exaggeration. In truth, it was no wider in places than a goat path. The muddy surface was pock-marked by shell holes and boulders that had rolled down from the surrounding cliffs.

"Better have a drink," said the driver, having reached under the seat for a thick brown bottle. He laughed merrily. "Who knows, it might be our last drink if those planes come back, ha, ha! Besides, it will keep us warm."

On the mountain road, the wind did, indeed, have a bitter edge.

The driver took a swig, one hand on the wheel and the other on the bottle, then offered it to the sour-faced young officer in the passenger seat beside him. The officer gave the driver a look as if he had just been offered horse dung.

"Keep your eyes on the road!" he snapped.

He was one of those serious young political officers, still zealous about the People's revolution and the fight against Imperialism. In other words, he was young and foolish. He had materialized two days before to escort Chen to the front.

Chastised by the young officer, the driver simply shrugged, then handed the bottle back over the seat to Chen.

Chen took the bottle and had a long drink, doing his best to keep the bottle from knocking out his front teeth as the driver tried, unsuccessfully, to avoid a crater in the road.

Chen gagged and sputtered, forcing the booze down.

"Ha, ha!" the driver shouted. "Good stuff."

Chen thought that whatever was in the bottle was hardly "good stuff." For all he knew, it might even be snake wine—derived from steeping a venomous snake in grain alcohol. No matter. In long years of war, first with the Japanese and then against the Nationalists and now against the United Nations, he had learned to be thankful for whatever was given.

He choked down another drink, hoping that this stuff wasn't actually snake whiskey, then handed the bottle back. The driver took it, laughing with delight, then returned his attention to the road. Chen hoped that the driver hadn't already imbibed too much of the alcohol, or their trip might be very short.

A few miles away, the Chinese were engaged in a vicious battle with United Nations forces that had become a stalemate. Chen was being called upon to shoot as many enemy soldiers as possible to help bring about an end to the stalemate—and to make the enemy pay dearly for each meter of ground.

He didn't normally think about politics, but even he had to admit that there was some opportunity here to prove to the haughty Americans that the Chinese were not only good shots, but maybe even better. Chen took pride in that thought.

Chen had to wonder if they would get there. The GAZ-67 was tough and reliable, but it was not the most agile vehicle. The Chinese nickname for them was *Lǎo lú* . . . the Old Donkey. Built in the Soviet Union, these vehicles had been shipped by the hundreds to the fight in North Korea. The sturdy vehicle was not fast, with a top speed of around 50 mph, and it most definitely was not comfortable—a fact to which Chen could attest to as he bounced around the back seat. The Chinese had not yet built a vehicle of their own because they did not have the facilities or the resources to make one, so they were forced to rely on Stalin's factories.

However, since the start of the war, the Chinese had become better at copying and making American weapons, such as the recoilless rifle. There was no need to make their own vehicles or tanks yet, as long as the Russians kept supplying them.

At the wheel of the vehicle, the driver used one hand to steer and the other to hang onto the bottle.

Overhead, the sky was a bright blue, framed by jagged mountains as they climbed ever-higher. The air felt cold, with the sun bringing little warmth to the deepest shadows. A cold wind blew and Chen did his best to ignore it. He was proud to be a Chinese soldier, and he knew that Chinese soldiers did not feel too cold or too hot, not like these soft Americans. A Chinese soldier endured.

Despite the cold, his spare blanket was not around his shoulders but instead was wrapped around his rifle. Considering the shortage of weapons, and the dubious quality of Chinese-made rifles, the Russian-made Moisin-Nagant was in some ways more valuable than Chen's life. He had tucked the rifle into the space near the floorboards to prevent it from bouncing out on the rough road. Instinctively, he reached down and stroked the rifle, in the same way that he might stroke a dog to calm it.

The young officer saw him and nodded approvingly. "Soon enough, you will get to use that rifle," he said. "But take good care of it! It is not your rifle, Chen. That rifle belongs to the people."

"It is a good rifle," Chang replied noncommittally. In reality, he knew well enough that the rifle was no more than a Russian hand-me-down. There was a simple scope that worked well enough for Chen, who had the eyes of an eagle. He wanted to ask the officer why he had gone to all the trouble of finding Chen and bringing him to this new battlefield, if the rifle was all that mattered.

"With tools such as this rifle, we shall defeat the imperialists," the young officer said.

Chen clenched his mouth shut, wondering if the officer really believed such nonsense, or if he was possibly testing Chen's loyalty. "Of course, sir."

"Remember that you are not important, Chen. You and I are not important. It is the mission that is important!"

The lieutenant looked pointedly at him, and Chen nodded as if the young officer was very wise. He wanted to respond that if the young officer cared so much about the mission and defeating imperialists, that he might consider getting out to fight the Americans instead of riding around uselessly in a vehicle, but he refrained from doing so. In Communist China, it was better to say as little as possible. They had thrown off the Japanese, and then Chiang Kai Shek's Nationalists, only to take on the yoke of the Communists.

Chen did not have strong political feelings. Like most Chinese, he simply wanted a better life for himself. He did not yet have children, but if some day he did, he wanted them to live in more peace and prosperity. The communists had promised new opportunity for all, but he was not yet convinced. There was still little enough food and almost no medical care. Now, there was this war. Sometimes, it seemed as if Chen had spent nearly his entire life fighting one enemy or another.

The driver looked over his shoulder and grunted. Another twist of the wheel in the driver's hand brought them perilously close to the edge of the road and the cliff beyond. Chen gulped.

This time, though, the driver hadn't swerved to avoid another pothole. Instead, the threat now came from the air. Already, he was driving a zigzagging pattern, trying to avoid being an easy target for the American planes.

How the driver had become aware of the planes was hard to say. The planes were still impossible to hear over the sound of the straining motor of the Gaz. Maybe the man had eyes in the back of his head. Once Chen turned his own head, his sharp eyes had no trouble spotting the threat. In the distance, two specks approached, sweeping in from the north. Enemy planes. Flying low, directly toward their vehicle.

"How many are there?" the young officer asked, scanning the sky.

"Two, coming in low on the horizon."

"No wonder you are a marksman," the officer said. "I can barely see those planes from here."

The planes closed the distance quickly. The screaming of the airplane engines could be heard distinctly over the GAZ-67 motor.

"Here they come!" the driver warned. "Hang on!"

"Faster!" the young officer shouted. Foolishly, he had drawn his pistol and was trying to aim it at the planes, but mostly pointing the muzzle at Chen as the vehicle bounced wildly.

"Put that away before you shoot one of us," Chen told him, recognizing that the officer was little more than a scared boy. "Do as the driver says and hang on."

The planes were United States Air Force Corsairs, prop-driven rather than the much faster Panther jets, but deadly nonetheless. Fast and nimble, they fell into formation behind the vehicle and swept in low and fast. At first, it was hard to hear them over the whine of their own vehicle's engine and the wind in their ears. But soon, the fighter planes were all that they could hear.

Up ahead, the road churned and boiled as the first Corsair strafed the surface with its .50 caliber machine guns. Luckily for them, the pilot's aim had been off. The plane swept past them and banked to the left, getting ready to turn and come at them again.

The driver yanked the wheel right, then left, trying to make the vehicle a difficult target. The front tires hit the rim of a pothole and suddenly the vehicle was airborne—Chen actually felt his behind lose contact with the seat. Then the GAZ crashed back down on all four tires with a bone-jarring rattle, never slowing down for an instant.

Would it do them any good? There was no hope of outrunning an airplane that could move at hundreds of miles per hour.

The second plane came at them now, flying as low as possible over the road. This pilot started firing early and walked the churning pattern of his strafing right toward them. It was like watching a falling tree coming right down on you. Chen closed his eyes and hunkered down in the back seat.

Bullets clipped the frame and punched holes in the sheet metal, sending bits of the GAZ flying everywhere. The driver screamed, but still struggled to keep control of the vehicle. He almost succeeded, but then the front tire hit another shell hole—or maybe it was shot out. The end result was that the sturdy vehicle finally slumped like a horse that had lost its front legs and began spinning sideways.

Overhead, the second plane screamed past and kept going, apparently satisfied that it had wreaked enough havoc.

Chen saw that the driver was slumped over the wheel, blood streaming from an ugly bullet hole in his neck. Chen tried to reach for the wheel, but it was too far away. Their only hope was for the officer in the passenger seat to regain control of the wheel, but he was frozen in fear, wailing in terror as the wheels of the GAZ finally lost contact with the road and the vehicle flipped through the air.

The last thing that Chen saw was the ground beneath him as the vehicle began to tumble end over end. And then his world went black.

CHAPTER FIVE

FOR A LONG TIME, Chen struggled in and out of consciousness. His mind became confused as he drifted through time and space. Suddenly, he was a child again, telling his brother to release him as they wrestled. *Let me go!* His brother was older and bigger, so he always had the advantage when they scuffled, as boys will do, constantly measuring their strength against the other.

Chen felt his legs being pinned down. Was his brother here? Chen's heart gladdened even in his mental confusion, for his brother had been dead for many years, murdered by the Japanese.

When he finally came to, he found himself hanging upside down under the Soviet-made vehicle. Tentatively, he tried to move his legs, half-expecting to be greeted by screaming pain. But to his surprise, his legs worked. He felt cuts and scrapes, but no major injuries.

Not that his entire body didn't hurt from the crash. But for the moment, he seemed to be whole.

His next concern was that he smelled a strong odor of gasoline. The fuel line must have ruptured during the accident. Thinking of fire, he fought back panic. He had seen men burn to death previously in similar accidents. He had to get out of here before something burst into flame.

Tugging at his legs, twisting and pulling, he extricated himself from the backseat, glad that he had not been pinned under the wreckage. Just ahead of him, he could see the driver who had been so jolly in life, generously sharing a bottle with Chen. It was clear that the weight of the vehicle had crushed the man—if the rounds from the American plane had not killed him outright before then.

The young officer was nowhere in sight.

Chen started to crawl away, then reached back and freed his rifle from where it was wedged under the back seats. Still wrapped in its protective blanket, the rifle appeared to be unharmed.

On his belly, Chen managed to worm his way free of the vehicle. Panting from the effort, he got to his hands and knees, but felt too dizzy to stand just yet. Looking around, he saw the young officer, who had been thrown clear of the wreck. A slight movement showed that the officer was still alive. Chen moved closer to see if he could give any assistance, but he saw that both the young man's legs were twisted at odd angles. A broken shaft of bone jutted from one leg. The young officer's legs had snapped like dry kindling.

"You must help me," the young officer said, struggling to speak through the pain.

Chen considered what to do. The vehicle was destroyed, which meant that the only option would be to build a litter of some sort to drag the officer along. He looked at the rough, winding road ahead and wondered how many miles they would need to cross.

Too many.

Looking down at the young officer, Chen shook his head. "You must rest here, sir. I will send help back for you."

"That will take hours!" the injured man complained. "You can't leave me here!"

Recalling the young officer's words to him earlier, Chen said: "Remember that we are not important, sir. You and I are not important. It is the mission that is important."

At that, Chen straightened up.

"What? You cannot leave me here like this!"

"I will send help," Chen reassured him. They both knew, of course,

that even if a patrol could be spared, by the time it reached this location there would only be a need to collect the bodies.

If there were any bodies left. In this remote mountain area, there
would likely be wolves or wild dogs scavenging once darkness fell.

The young officer seemed to be having much the same thought.
"Don't leave me!" he cried, using his hands to tug at his legs, as if trying
to arrange them into working order. They flopped uselessly. The effort
caused the officer to whimper in pain.

"You have your pistol if you need it, sir," Chen said. He did not
elaborate on the fact that, like a wounded horse, the officer might need
to put himself out of his own misery.

Ignoring the young officer's protests, Chen started up the road on
foot. Thankfully, the American planes were long since gone.

The American pilots could not have known that they were
targeting the vehicle carrying a celebrated enemy sniper to the battlefield, but their attack had been more than effective. Already, the
mission to bring Chen to the battlefield had cost the lives of
two men.

Nothing else moved on the road, although other wrecked vehicles
indicated that many other Chinese troops had met the same fate due
to the airplanes. Chen wouldn't mind shooting one of them down, one
of these days, for some small measure of revenge against the imperialists.

Finally, he stood up, reeling. He must have hit his head in the crash.
Considering that he was still alive, however, he had nothing to
complain about.

Shouldering the bundled rifle, he began to make his way down the
road, limping. In the distance, he could hear the thump of artillery,
which meant that he must not be more than a few miles from his
destination.

Sometimes, it seemed as if Chen had been fighting his whole life. If
he'd had any sense, he might have slipped away into the mountains.
Surely, there must be someplace he could sit out the rest of the war.

But running away was not in Chen's nature. Resolutely, he put one
foot in front of the other, marching toward the sound of the fighting.

Suddenly, he heard the sound of the American planes returning, scorching their way across the blue skies in a blur of speed. They were coming back to finish the job that they had started.

Chen didn't even bother to look over his shoulder. This time, the planes were not strafing the road, but were using rockets. He heard the first rocket hit the road near the wreckage of the vehicle. He put his head down and ran to hide among the rocks at the side of the road.

* * *

ONCE THE AMERICAN planes had gone again, leaving more pockmarks on the mountain road, Chen moved on toward the sound of the fighting. He walked all the rest of the day and as dusk neared, the crackling cold settled in, sinking its claws into exposed flesh.

Chen approached the Chinese position, taking stock in the dim light. What he saw was not encouraging. It was true that the Chinese occupied the high ground, but their positions had been heavily shelled by the Americans. Everywhere that Chen looked, he saw churned earth, shattered trees, and ground plowed by enemy artillery. Wherever there was a ditch or trench, it was occupied by troops, who looked cold despite their padded uniforms. Originally white or light gray, these uniforms were now almost universally a brown color from caked mud and the filth of living close to the ground in order to avoid the American shelling. Faces stared back at him, some curiously, but most of the faces remained expressionless. Chinese soldiers were used to simply enduring and they knew better than to ask questions.

Despite passing several sentries, none bothered to stop him or ask his business, but why should they? He was clearly Chinese, which meant that he was not the enemy. Also, the sniper rifle he carried was as good as a special pass or an officer's insignia.

The enemy was down in the valley below, trying to displace the Chinese with their endless supply of artillery shells. So far, the Chinese had held—just barely. The desperate faces that Chen had seen showed him just how close his comrades were to the breaking point.

When the Americans stopped shelling and when darkness came to protect them from the American planes, the Chinese attacked in force. They had not yet managed to displace the Americans.

Back and forth, the two sides went. They had reached a stalemate, and a stalemate never made the officers happy.

And so they had sent for Chen.

He and his rifle could create a wedge of fear that even the big guns could not provide. The sooner that he struck, the better. He was reminded of an old proverb that advised, *the first blow is half the battle.*

Having reached the Chinese lines, he was soon able to find the headquarters. Not long after that, he was called before Major Wu, whom he had met before during the Chosin Reservoir campaign against the imperialists. Chen trusted Wu about as much as one might trust a hungry wolf, but he had no choice in the matter, considering that it must have been Wu who had summoned Chen here in the first place.

The major looked him up and down, grinning all the while. He was not outwardly serious like the young lieutenant had been, but Chen knew that the good humor was a mask.

"Where is Lieutenant Huang?" the major asked.

Chen shook his head. "He is dead, sir. We were attacked on the road by American planes." Chen did not bother to explain that the lieutenant had still been alive when Chen had left him. Perhaps he had been killed in the second attack by the American planes. If he had lived, and the mountain wolves or wild dogs had not gotten to the lieutenant by now, they would soon. If the lieutenant had been smart, he would have shot himself. Better to die swiftly than to suffer in the chill of the mountain night, or worse.

Major Wu nodded, still grinning. He wore the perpetual smile that made him resemble a *shishi*, one of the traditional Chinese guardian lions. "That Huang, he was too full of himself, anyhow. What matters is that you are here now. First, we must get you a better uniform. One that is not covered in mud and blood, anyhow."

The major shouted for an aide, explained what he wanted, and sent him on his errand. While he was gone, the major chatted pleasantly with Chen, wanting to know something of his childhood and details of his military service. He seemed pleased that Chen had fought against the Japanese and that he had received some of his sniper training from

German advisors, back before they had become allied with the armies of the Rising Sun.

"The Germans were very good snipers," Chen said. He wished that he had one of their rifles equipped with a finely made telescopic sight, but he knew better than to complain. The old Moisin-Nagant was as good as it was going to get for him.

"From what I have seen, they taught you well," Wu said.

Then, the aide was back, panting as if he had been running the whole time. He presented Chen with a pristine new uniform.

"I took this from the field hospital," he explained. "The soldier it belonged to won't be needing it anymore."

Wu made a face. "I hope that he did not die from something contagious."

"Sir, I could find another uniform—"

"Never mind that!" Major Wu said impatiently, sending the aide out. He turned to Chen. "Put that on, and come with me."

Chen did as he was told, quickly changing into the fresh uniform and trying not to dwell on how it had managed to stay so pristine if its original owner was dead. His old uniform was tossed into a heap— dirty, smelling of gasoline, and spattered with blood that Chen had not noticed before—more than likely, it was the blood of the dead driver.

When he followed the major out of the tent, he was amazed to see that hundreds of soldiers had been assembled outside. Chen moved to take his place in the ranks, but Major Wu caught him by the elbow. "Where are you going, Chen?" he asked, appearing to be amused, grinning widely once again. "You stay right here. Hold your rifle up so that everyone may see it!"

It was then that Chen realized he was to be put on display. He froze with fear worse than he had ever felt on the battlefield. A sniper was someone who kept to the shadows, after all.

He stood at attention, holding his rifle in the present arms position until his arms ached, while the major gave a long-winded speech about how the Chinese army would soon be defeating the United Nations forces—mainly the American army—in no time at all now that the famed sniper Chen Li was here on the battlefield.

Major Wu turned to him, his eyes blazing with the excitement of the moment. "You will turn the tide of battle single-handedly!" Behind Wu, other officers raised their arms as a signal for the soldiers to cheer. As the sound swelled up to fill the gathering darkness, Chen felt ill and overwhelmed.

To add to his discomfort, a uniformed photographer stepped forward and took a flash photo, leaving Chen blinded.

He was no people's hero, just a man with a rifle. But looking around at his comrades, hope finally evident on their faces, he turned to Wu. "Please, sir. This is an honor that I do not deserve."

"Do not be so selfish," Wu said, smiling out at the crowd, but addressing Chen. "You are thinking only of yourself right now. Do not deny them a hero."

Chen realized that he was in no position to argue. He raised the rifle half-heartedly over his head, and the gathered soldiers cheered.

CHAPTER SIX

WHILE CHEN WAS RECEIVING accolades in the Chinese headquarters several mountain ridges away, Cole was hauling buckets of dirty gray dishwater to be dumped on the hard-packed ground outside the mess tent.

"Get your ass in gear!" shouted Sergeant Springer, the grizzled NCO who ran the mess tent. He had greeted Cole on his first morning by throwing a dirty apron at him, and then put him to work reconstituting powdered eggs that were then heated up on a griddle. Cooking for an army in the field was about quantity, not quality. By six a.m., the sight and smell of the reconstituted eggs had Cole feeling sick to the stomach.

There was an old saying down South that you should never trust a skinny cook. Judging by the belly on Sergeant Springer, there wasn't any danger of him not inspiring trust in his cooking—so long as you didn't mind a few cigar ashes in your scrambled eggs or in your mashed potatoes. Short, squat, chewing a cigar stub, and gloriously profane, he was like a cross between Chef Tell and Napoleon.

Sergeant Springer barked a lot, but he didn't bite so long as you worked hard, which is exactly what Cole did. The kitchen was a cramped space, with a long galley of cooking stoves and work tables separated by a narrow aisle. Unlike some of the field kitchens in WWII that had dirt or grass floors, this one had an actual wooden floor of rough-sawn boards. The boards had come from a dismantled Korean barn.

Kitchen duty was about what Cole expected. He found himself assigned all of the grunt duty. After the eggs, he set about opening endless Number 10 cans of green beans and peaches and beans. He plunged around in vats of greasy gray dishwater, scrubbing pots and utensils to some degree of cleanliness, or at least, cleaner than they were.

He might even have been able to tolerate the work for the duration of the war if it hadn't been for Tater Kelly. He was just a cook, a private like Cole, but he lorded it over the kitchen help like a five-star general.

"I got my eye on you," was what Tater said to Cole by way of introduction. "You best do whatever I tell you."

Tater was the bully in the kitchen. He pushed, he shoved, he browbeat. Sgt. Springer either didn't notice or didn't care because Tater didn't give him any trouble.

It was hard to say how Tater got his nickname other than that he looked like a big spud. He was a huge guy, six-foot-two, around two-hundred and eighty pounds—with most of it in a beer belly and massive biceps. If the mess hall chief demanded nothing but hard work, Tater did whatever he could to make sure someone else did his work for him—when the chief wasn't looking.

Cole's new strategy was to lay low and stay out of trouble. He was done with being a soldier. Lieutenant Ballard had beaten him down one too many times. Peeling potatoes was fine with him. With any luck, he could wait out his two years in Korea in the kitchen. He might never have to go on the battlefield again. By the end of that first day, however, he realized that Tater was going to seriously spoil his plans.

Tater was a bully who picked on everyone in the kitchen, but he had it in for Cole the minute he laid eyes on him. For his part, Cole kept hoping that Tater would leave him alone once Cole wasn't the new guy anymore, but the big fool seemed to have it in for Cole, zeroing in on his mountain accent.

"Hillbilly, must be strange for you to wear shoes, huh?" or "Hey, you know what they call a hillbilly girl who can outrun her brothers? A virgin!"

It was odd how the name "Hillbilly" just seemed to follow him around. Cole supposed it was his accent.

Cole could take the name-calling and the jokes, but he drew the line when Tater got physical.

The first time was when Cole was carrying a big pot of soup, hot off the stove, to the mess hall itself. Cole struggled with the heavy pot, navigating the narrow aisles and dodging other men busy with their tasks. He knew that he'd catch hell from the mess chief if he spilled so much as a single drop.

Just as Cole was in the home stretch, headed for the door into the mess hall, someone shoved him from behind. Cole staggered, fighting to keep the soup from spilling, but he was only partly successful. Soup splashed everywhere: the floor, the walls of the tent, and all over Cole. It didn't help that the soup had been boiling on the stove less than a minute before.

The spilled soup had not escaped the cook's attention. "God-dammit!" he shouted, so angry that he plucked the damp stump of the cigar from between his lips. "Can't you even carry a pot of soup without spilling it? You are fucking useless! Now get that out to the mess hall and then get back in here and clean up this fucking mess! Goddammit!"

"Yes, sir." Cole felt sheepish for spilling the soup and drawing the mess chief's ire. But it hadn't been entirely his fault. He looked around and saw Tater leaning against a stainless steel counter, snickering. The other kitchen staff was looking from Tater to Cole, wondering what would happen. If Sergeant Springer had seen what happened, he had chosen to take it out on Cole and not his right-hand man in the kitchen.

"What's a matter, Hillbilly?" Tater asked. "Not used to wearing shoes?"

Cole glared at him. "That's once."

"What, do I get three strikes? What happens then?"

Cole didn't answer, but just struggled into the mess hall with the heavy pot, blinking soup out of his eyes.

* * *

COLE GOT through most of the next two days without trouble from Tater, but he should have known that wasn't going to last. Meanwhile, he turned his attention to the other staff. He really had it in for African-American guys, calling them all sorts of names. They glowered at him, but that was just about all that they could do. The Army was no longer segregated, but that didn't mean a black man had equal say.

Tired from a day in the kitchen, Cole let his guard down. He was carrying a tray of dirty dishes when he felt the massive shove from behind. The tray—and Cole—went flying. He found himself down on his hands and knees, dirty utensils were strewn across the floor and getting under everyone's feet.

"Goddammit!" shouted the mess hall chief. "Pick that shit up!"

Tater stood nearby, grinning at Cole like the cat that ate the canary.

"That's twice," Cole said.

"Let's see how high you can count, you dumb hillbilly," Tater said, and kicked a pile of utensils under a stove, where they would be hard to reach.

Cole seriously considered taking a carving knife to Tater and skinning him out. He was that angry. But Tater would have welcomed a brawl. In the tight space, his size gave him every advantage, and he was the biggest guy in the kitchen.

What Tater didn't know was that Cole had already been thinking up a plan. He'd been a trapper in the mountains, and he knew how to set a good trap. He had a piece of cord in his pocket that he'd been trying to figure how to use.

Down on his hands and knees, Cole came up with a plan. He scuttled among the legs of guys busy making hamburger or mashing potatoes, hunting up the stray utensils. He also took a moment to tie one end of the cord to the heavy leg of a cook stove. The cord went into a crack in a floor board where it would be out of the way, across the narrow aisle to the stainless steel counter, where he snaked it up a leg of the counter and knotted it so that it wedged in the corner where the rim of the counter came together. One good yank and the cord would stretch tight across the aisle.

Cole finished cleaning up the utensils and got back to work. Fortunately, it was toward the end of the day. He'd held his temper in check
enough for one day. It didn't help that whenever Tater caught his eye in
the kitchen, the big man was laughing at him.

Laugh while you can, Cole thought.

* * *

THE NEXT MORNING, Cole was back in the kitchen for another day of
endless chores. The Army was a funny thing, he decided. You could sit
out in a foxhole all day and literally do nothing except get shot at from
time to time, or you could do all sorts of menial, exhausting work all
day in the kitchen, but not have to worry about getting shot.

Cole was not complaining. He thought about Pomeroy and the kid
out there on the line. He felt kind of bad that he wasn't there with
them, but that was the old Caje Cole. The new Caje Cole worked in
the kitchen, keeping his head down and counting the days until his
time in the service was up.

It would all have been fine if it hadn't been for that goddamn Tater.
That bully just couldn't leave well enough alone. He seemed to leave
Cole alone just long enough to torment the others in the kitchen. As
soon as he could, Cole checked to make sure that the cord he had tied
in place yesterday was still there. Reassured that one good tug would
pull the cord taut across the narrow galley aisle, he got back to work.

Just after lunch detail, Cole was slinging the mop around over the
rough-cut floorboards in the galley between the stoves and counters,
trying to get up the worst of the grease. The task wasn't made easier by
the fact that the space was narrow and hard to maneuver. Just about
everything cooked in that kitchen was greasy in one form or another:
bacon and hamburger, mostly. So much of that grease got on the floor
over a couple of days that it was actually a slipping hazard.

When the mess hall chief went out, Tater had free reign. He helped
himself to a cup of coffee and then smacked a couple of the African-
American guys in the head for no other reason than to torment them.
He followed up by calling them lazy—and worse. They didn't have any
choice but to take it.

Then he made his way up the narrow galley to where Cole was mopping and, without warning, kicked over the bucket that stood between them. The sudsy, gray, greasy water sloshed everywhere.

"Oh, now you've done it, you dumb hillbilly. If I were you, I'd get mopping faster before the Old Man comes back in."

Cole hit him in the face with the dirty mop.

Tater stood for a moment in shock because he began to sputter and curse, spitting the filthy water out of his mouth and wiping it from his face.

"Taste good?" Cole asked.

"You're dead, Hillbilly!"

Like a bull, the big man charged up the aisle after Cole, who barely had time to get out of the way. For his size, Tater was awfully quick— or maybe his anger had made him swift. Cole tossed the mop aside to free his hands.

Cole stepped over the cord that lay tucked into a crack in the board, with Tater hot on his heels. He grabbed for the knot tucked into the steel counter to his right and pulled it tight, hoping that there was enough distance between them for it to do any good. If Tater caught him, Cole had to admit that the much larger man was likely to beat him to a pulp.

The cord pulled taught. The big man tripped.

Tater went down hard.

One second he was barreling after Cole like a steaming locomotive, and the next second he was hitting the floor like the proverbial sack of potatoes.

Cole didn't give him a chance to get back up. He didn't plan on fighting fair.

Instead, he grabbed an oversized cast iron skillet off the stove and clobbered Tater over the head with it. One-handed. If he'd used two hands, the blow would have cracked the other man's skull like an egg and killed him. Tater screamed, not so much from the blow as from the fact that the skillet was full of sizzling bacon fat that was now oozing over his head and shoulders. Still on his hands and knees, Tater clawed and swiped at the dripping grease.

Cole let go of the skillet, letting it clatter to the floor. As far as he was concerned, he was done with Tater.

But the others were just getting started.

To Cole's surprise, the other kitchen staff that Tater had tormented moved in. He caught sight of two of the African-American cooks, one carrying a big two-pronged fork used for handling chunks of meat. Both men had murder in their eyes. Before Cole could open his mouth to speak, the fork jabbed down, again and again, as if Tater was a juicy roast beef. Tater cried out in agony as the fork plunged into his plump bits. Two more cooks jumped in, kicking and stomping the fallen bully for all they were worth.

"All right, that's enough," Cole said half-heartedly. "Don't go killing him."

Nobody was listening. The blows continued. Cole shrugged. Nobody could say that Tater didn't have it coming.

That's when the mess chief walked back in. He stared in astonishment at the violent scene before him. His mouth fell open and his cigar actually fell out. His mouth opened and closed, but no words came out. For once, he seemed to be caught speechless.

The beating continued until the chief managed to boom at the top of his lungs, "Knock it off!"

Cole wiped his hands on the apron and picked up the mop. When Tater finally came around, Cole figured his days in the mess tent would be over.

Somebody ran to fetch a medic.

Staring down at the groaning mess, Cole said, "Looks to me like Tater has done been mashed." He then went back to mopping the floor, humming tunelessly to himself.

CHAPTER SEVEN

COLE'S only respite from working in the kitchen was the pup tent that he shared with the kid, Tommy Wilson. Pomeroy snored something awful, and Cole was a light sleeper, so he had made sure that he was in a different tent. Pomeroy's tentmate was a former artilleryman who was deaf as a post.

The tent that Cole shared with the kid wasn't much more than basic shelter, formed by two canvas shelter halves that buttoned together along the ridge line. There wasn't any floor. When they were on the march, each man carried one half of the tent with him, including one of the three-piece wooden tent poles and a handful of tent pegs. There wasn't any floor, so they had dug a shallow trench around the tent to keep the water out when it rained. The interior smelled strongly of canvas, waterproofing wax, mildew, and both bedding and bodies that needed a wash. Home sweet home.

The battle over these Korean hills had reached the point where it was actually more of a siege over the past few weeks, so some of the support structures—like the mess hall—were semi-permanent. Even some of the officers had wall tents that were roomier and thus moderately more comfortable. Some of the officers had actual stoves to heat their tents. The men in Cole's unit made do with their Army pup tents.

It was getting too cold to sit outside, and worse than that, there was always the danger of an enemy sniper. The enemy occasionally crept within range to harass the American troops, keeping them on edge. This was yet another way that the enemy was trying to wear them down.

Cole was beginning to think that the Chinese snipers were as bad as the Germans in that regard. More than a few GIs had been picked off while lighting up a smoke or simply walking too close to the battle-field. Consequently, Cole kept to the tent. It beat getting frostbite—or ending up in somebody's crosshairs.

There really wasn't room to sit upright inside the tent, but you could sort of prop yourself up on an elbow to read or maybe write a letter, which was exactly what the kid was doing now.

It just so happened that a few days before, Cole had received a letter of his own from back home. He was fairly certain who it was from. Much as he would have liked to know what it said, the envelope remained shoved deep into his pocket. Cole could tell time by the sun, start a fire with nothing more than a bit of flint and his knife, field strip a rifle, and shoot anything that his keen eyes could see, but he couldn't read or write more than a handful of basic words.

Heaving a sigh, the kid put aside his pencil and paper in frustration.

"I don't know what to write to my parents," the kid said. "How many times can I write home that everything is fine, when it's not? I feel like I'm just lying to them."

Cole thought about that.

"Kid, your folks just want to hear that you are OK," he said. "Put in there that the food is great and that you like the scenery. Telling a few white lies like that in a letter home never hurt no one."

"I suppose you're right. I'm also going to send a letter to this girl I knew back home. We went to the fortnightly dances together a few times." He sighed. "I never know what to write to her, either. What should I say?"

Cole considered this new question. "Tell her what a good time you had when you went out, and what you love about her."

"Like about her," the kid said, correcting him. Even in the dim light inside the tent, it was clear that his face was turning red.

Cole smiled. "You made love to her yet?"

"What? You mean like—" the kid paused, aghast at the thought. He turned an even deeper shade of red. "When would I have done that? There were chaperones at all the dances."

Cole shook his head. "We're a funny society, kid. We think it's all right to send our teenage boys to war, maybe bayonet somebody to death, but God forbid they should kiss a girl at a dance. Ought to be the other way around, if'n you ask me. When you get back, you can do things the right way."

"Why don't you ever get any letters?" the kid asked. "I've never seen you write one, either."

Cole grunted.

He wondered if maybe he had made a mistake tenting up with the kid rather than Pomeroy, who seemed to know better than to ask a lot of questions. Mostly, Pomeroy just crawled into the tent and went to sleep. Then again, there was that godawful snoring.

It just so happened that a few days before, he had, in fact, received a letter from back home. Unopened, this was the letter that now felt like a hot coal burning a hole in his pocket.

Should he tell the kid about it?

Receiving mail was something of an unusual event for Cole. He knew who this letter was from. He could make out enough words to recognize the return address in Gashey's Creek. He could also puzzle out the name: Norma Jean Elwood. It was Norma Jean whom he had rescued from a couple of hard cases, resulting in them getting shot and Cole reenlisting to avoid being sent to prison.

There wasn't nothing happy about that story, he reflected.

She had written him once before, thanking him for his actions and wishing him good luck, and also stating that she would like to see him when he got home from the war. This last possibility intrigued Cole, but he had not written back. Mostly because he didn't know how.

He had gotten the kid to read that letter to him, claiming that he was too seasick to read it. Cole was a confident man in most regards, afraid of nothing and no one, but he felt embarrassed about his lack of education. There hadn't been much in the way of school back home in the mountains, and no one much cared if he went or not, anyhow. Back then, book learning hadn't meant a hill of beans to Cole, but he was starting to change his mind about that.

Meanwhile, the letter in his pocket felt like it was burning hotter.

To hell with it, he thought, and dug the letter out of his pocket.

"What's that?" the kid asked, clearly surprised by the sight of the envelope in his hands.

"It just so happens that I did get some mail." Cole paused. "I was wondering if you would read it to me."

"Read it to you? Why—" Realization dawned on Tommy's face. He seemed to know better than to push it. "Oh. Sure, I can read it to you if you want."

Cole handed over the letter.

"Norma Jean Elwood, huh? She's got nice handwriting." "Just read it," Cole snapped.

Tommy cleared his throat and began reading:

Dear Caje,

I hope that you are doing fine. We read in the newspapers about all the trouble that the Army had fighting the Chinese at that frozen reservoir, so I hope that you weren't part of that mess. We are getting back into fall and the nights are getting cool. You can smell the smoke from chimneys and the leaves are changing colors. The other night I heard a Great Horned Owl out hunting, and it was such a lonely sound that for some reason made me think of you and write this here letter. Things has been quiet regarding that business we was involved in, so everything should be fine when you get home. You never wrote me back, so maybe you aren't interested, but I hope to see you when you get home from Korea.

Your friend,
Norma Jean Elwood

. . .

THE KID WAS GRINNING. "I'll be darned. You've got a girlfriend back home. You never wrote her back?"

"How would I do that?"

"I have a pencil and paper right here. Why don't you let me do it, on account of your battle wounds."

"My what?"

"You'll see."

With the kid's help, Cole composed a letter home to Norma Jean. He provided the words, with a flourish or two from the kid. One of these flourishes included the fact that it turned out that Cole hadn't written back because he got frostbite in his fingers during that fight at the reservoir that Norma Jean had mentioned.

"That's a lie," Cole pointed out.

"A white lie. You just said that sometimes those are all right."

Cole shook his head. The kid had him, there, although that wasn't exactly what he'd had in mind when he had mentioned white lies.

The letter ended with the words he asked the kid to put down, *I'll be sure to see you when I get home.*

For some reason, those words made him know exactly how that lonely owl had felt.

The kid addressed the envelope and handed it to Cole. "You can send that out in the morning." He hesitated. "You can send mine, too."

Tommy hadn't said a word about it, but Cole sensed that the kid was anxious about something, and for good reason. In the morning, the unit was slated to go back on the line. They had been out there before, keeping a wary eye on the enemy occupying Sniper Ridge, but rumors were flying that this was going to be different because an attack on the Chinese was being planned. To prepare, the kid began cleaning his rifle—or attempting to, anyway, because he was having trouble reassembling the M-1. He would have thought the kid would know that rifle inside out by now, but his fingers fumbled the task, either from cold or from the nervousness about what was to come tomorrow.

Cole watched him for a while. If the kid asked for help, he'd help him. Cole had helped him with that rifle as far back as boot camp. But sometimes, you had to figure things out for yourself, because that was how you learned. Cole had always believed that if you wanted something done right, then you should do it yourself.

His own well-oiled rifle lay next to his sleeping bag, where he had left it days ago. There wasn't much need for a rifle in the kitchen.

While the rest of the unit would be heading into combat, Cole had orders to stay behind in the kitchen. He was just fine with sitting out this fight, anyhow. To his surprise, the mess hall chief must have liked the job that Cole was doing. The sergeant didn't even seem to suspect that Cole had been the one who had beaten the hell out of Tater. Or maybe he did know, and figured that Tater had it coming.

Finally, Tommy tossed away the pieces of the rifle in frustration.

"Goddammit!" the kid muttered, which was unusual. He didn't swear much, at least not by Army standards.

"Give it here a minute," Cole said, holding out his hand.

The kid handed over the rifle, and Cole deftly clicked the stock, barrel, and trigger mechanism into place. He took the kid's oily rag and gave the weapon a good wipe down.

"Thanks, Cole," Tommy said, watching Cole's expert hands. "You're good at that."

"This ain't my first rodeo, kid."

"I know that you were in the last war, too. Hell, you were at D-Day. Tell me about it."

"It ain't exactly a bedtime story," Cole said. He continued wiping down the rifle, doing so almost lovingly. "Besides, there ain't much to tell."

"Were you scared?"

Cole glanced at him. So that's what was eating at the kid. Cole could understand—going into battle was not an experience that any man took lightly. "Hell, kid, only a fool ain't scared. But you know the drill. It ain't your first rodeo, either."

"It's not something I'll ever get used to."

"Just keep your head down and listen to what Sergeant Weber tells you. Most of these young officers have got their heads up their ass, Lieutenant Ballard included, but Weber knows what's going on."

"Good advice."

Cole handed back the rifle and clapped him on the shoulder. "You'll be all right, kid."

"If you say so. What was it like for you, the first time? Bet you weren't even scared."

"Just to be clear, we are talking about battle, right, and not about something else?"

The kid blushed again. "Battle."

Cole nodded, thinking it over. In a sense, he had gotten his baptism by fire long before the war.

As a boy, Cole had once hunted down and killed a bootlegger who was trying to do the same to him, but he knew that wasn't what Tommy meant. The kid was asking him about Omaha Beach at H-hour on June 6, 1944.

"I reckon I wasn't scared as much as I was angry at them Germans," he said, leaving out the part where a German machine gun had killed his buddy from boot camp, Jimmy Turner, within minutes of them hitting the beach. It was Jimmy who had first painted a Confederate flag on his helmet. Cole had one painted on his helmet here in Korea as a good luck charm.

The kid didn't need to hear all that. "I was mad as hell at the Germans for shooting at us. Don't make much sense now that I'm saying it, but there you have it. Got my dander up."

The kid grinned. "I'd like to see that."

"You might not."

"Did you shoot anyone right away?" Tommy asked, his grin fading.

"Everybody was shooting," Cole replied. "It would have been hard not to shoot someone."

"Cole, I saw you on the range back at boot camp. You couldn't hit the broad side of a barn door. Everyone in the squad knew that. But you got to Korea and you became the best shot in the unit. Like you had done this before. What was that all about?"

Earlier, Cole had managed to hide his past as a sniper from the others in the unit. To them, he was just the hillbilly who worked in the kitchen. Circumstances had put a rifle back in his hands. But now, Lieutenant Ballard had sent him back to the kitchen.

Something in Cole's eyes made the kid look away. His stare sent shivers down the kid's spine.

"I wish you were going with us tomorrow," the kid said.

"You'll be fine," Cole said, wishing that he believed it.

CHAPTER EIGHT

FOR POMEROY AND TOMMY WILSON, morning came far too soon, after a restless and fitful night. Even exhaustion proved itself to be a poor balm against the rough edges of fear that haunted their dreams. They were up before dawn, eating a hurried breakfast of cold rations, and then herded into position. Cole had already gone off to the mess tent, far from the front line.

Pomeroy and the kid weren't quite so lucky. They were going into battle.

The trouble was, they were going to be attacking the Chinese position today, in an effort to drive the enemy off Sniper Ridge. Judging by the defenses up there, a lot of them wouldn't be coming back.

"Just like cattle to the slaughter. I don't like this kid," Pomeroy said. "Not one bit."

"We don't have much choice," the kid responded, putting his head down and shrinking back into his own thoughts. Pomeroy was sure that those thoughts were far from this godforsaken patch of Korean real estate—he sure knew his own thoughts kept returning to home. Back during the Chosin Reservoir campaign, they had actually thought that they might all get home for Christmas. That had been months ago, and here they all still were.

Nobody was talking about being home for Christmas this time around.

Home hadn't been all that great for Pomeroy. He had a wife who wasn't all that happy to see him come back from Europe in the first place, a couple of kids that he hadn't connected with very well because he'd been off at war when they were born, and a job in a factory. It paid OK, but he had always hoped for something better.

"You know, it's funny," he mused out loud. "I was itching to get back into the army just because I was bored and things weren't going so well at home, you know. Now, I can't wait to get back there."

"You're not the only one," the kid agreed.

"The sooner we win this war, then the sooner we get back," Pomeroy said. "With any luck, maybe that starts today."

He attempted to inject some enthusiasm into his voice, both for his benefit and for Tommy's. It wasn't easy. Pomeroy's joints ached and his back felt stiff from the night's cold and having slept on the ground, even if it had been inside the pup tent.

Sometimes he felt as if he had never really warmed all the way up after the Chosin Reservoir. He still had nightmares about how the cold clawed at him. That same cold had claimed some of his toes and an even larger chunk of his spirit. Somehow though, he kept going. That was what his soldier did after all, and he put a brave face on it if for no other reason than to reassure the kid walking beside him.

His wounds from the mess at Chosin would have been enough to get him sent home if he had talked them up. Instead, he had talked his way back into the field. This morning, that seemed like a mistake.

"I wish Cole was here," the kid said.

"Yeah, well, you'll just have to make do with me."

"I didn't mean—"

"I know what you meant, kid," Pomeroy said.

Pomeroy didn't want to admit it, but he wished Cole was here, too. He was a good man to have watching your back in a fight. He had yet to see the man afraid. That hillbilly had ice water running through his veins. Not for the first time, he was glad that they were on the same side.

All around them in the gray dawn light, other soldiers were moving into position. Units were converging from all directions on the ridge ahead. Again, Pomeroy didn't like the looks of this. It was shaping up to be a big attack.

In a big attack, lots of men tended to get killed.

Off to their rear, he could see that the artillery gunners were set up and ready to go. Some lounged by their guns, smoking and waiting. All they needed was a signal.

The purpose of an artillery bombardment would be to soften up the enemy, but Pomeroy thought that you might as well just hold up a big sign that announced to the enemy: *Here we come.*

From what he had seen, the artillery never did a whole lot of good because those Chinese and North Korean bastards always managed to dig themselves deep into the ridge.

They were climbing now, moving up the steep hillside. He could hear the heavy breathing and curses of the soldiers struggling around him. In the semi-darkness, Pomeroy managed to stumble over every stone and pothole imaginable. His missing toes did not help with his footing, either. *Dammit*, he muttered, stumbling, but kept right on going. Not that he had any choice.

"Tighten it up and move along," urged the sergeant.

Sergeant Weber was all business this morning and for good reason; clearly he felt the nervousness of the men, and even as an old combat veteran, he still looked plenty apprehensive himself. One sign was that old Weber wouldn't look anybody in the eye.

They climbed higher, spreading out along the top of the ridge. When they finally reached the apex, Pomeroy noticed that the ridge was topped by two distinct rocky knobs. Some had taken to calling these knobs Mao's Ears, but to Pomeroy's mind, they almost like a giant gunsight overlooking the Chinese position. It was one hell of an ominous landmark, he thought. He and the kid found themselves being placed right between those ears.

"Check your rifle, kid," he said quietly. "Make sure it's loaded and keep your bayonet handy. I hope to hell it doesn't come to that, but you never know. We've been through this before."

"Yeah," the kid said. "I'll never forget those fights." The kid was referring to the retreat from the Chosen Reservoir. "I didn't think we'd get out of that one alive."

"Hell, I didn't think we'd ever thaw out again," Pomeroy said, huffing for breath. He was feeling winded from the hike up the hill. Not for the first time, he regretted smoking so much. He wasn't about to give up cigarettes this morning, though. He was going to need a smoke in a bit to calm his nerves.

They reached the ridge and got into position. All up and down the line, Pomeroy could see men in position. This was shaping up to be a full-scale attack. He almost felt sorry for the Chinese somewhere ahead of them. They were about to get a rude awaking this morning.

"Smoke 'em if you got 'em," the sergeant said. "We don't go until after the artillery gives them a thumping."

Gratefully, Pomeroy lit a cigarette. He couldn't help but notice that his hands were shaking as he held up the lighter, being careful to keep his head down as he did so. There were always a few Chinese snipers around, and they might already be at work. Again, he would have felt better about Chinese snipers if Cole had been there. He was like their secret weapon. But right now, he was back down in the mess tent, scrubbing pots and pans. It was a goddamn waste of talent, considering what a good shot Cole was with a rifle.

If you asked Pomeroy, it was all Lieutenant Ballard's fault for giving Cole's rifle to somebody else. Ballard claimed it was simply a matter of allotting limited equipment, but Pomeroy knew better. The lieutenant didn't like it that Cole wouldn't lick his boots. Ballard's designated sniper, Heywood, must be good at boot licking. There was also the fact that Cole was a dyed-in-the-wool hillbilly, which didn't sit well with Ballard.

The lieutenant came walking up the line now, apparently intending to impart a few words of wisdom. He was the only man who didn't look nervous this morning. In fact, he looked well-rested in a clean uniform, as if he had gotten a solid night's sleep. Trailing in the lieutenant's wake was the new sniper, carrying the rifle that should rightfully be Cole's. Like Ballard, this sniper looked as if he'd been sleeping a little too well. He held the scoped rifle casually—not even so far as looking in the direction of the Chinese lines. Pomeroy suspected that Cole would have been in location before dawn.

Taking up a position where he could address most of the men, Ballard drew himself up to his full height and put his hands on his hips. He then raised his voice to be heard up and down the line.

"When we hit them, I want you to hit them hard," he said. "Let's show the enemy what we're made of, boys. Let's show them how Americans fight!"

A ragged shout came from the line.

Pomeroy muttered, "What the hell else would we do? Play patty cakes with the Chinese?"

The kid snickered. "Jeez, don't let the lieutenant hear you say that, or he'll make you lead the attack."

"You're brighter than you look, kid," Pomeroy said. "You're finally catching on to this army business."

But the lieutenant's gaze sought out Pomeroy, as if maybe he had heard him, after all.

"Private, I want you to be Heywood's spotter," the lieutenant said. "You've had some experience with that, I believe."

"Yes, sir." Under his breath, Pomeroy added, "Nuts to that."

The lieutenant was glaring at Pomeroy as if maybe he had read his lips. He opened his mouth to bark something at him, but the lieutenant's words were lost in the rolling *boom* that swept the battlefield.

Lucky for Pomeroy, the artillery had picked that moment to open fire. The concussion of the big guns seemed to suck the air out of his lungs, even at this distance. The soldiers on the ridge covered their ears. It was no wonder that you could always tell an artilleryman—he was the guy talking too loud because he was so damn deaf. The smell of cordite drifted over them.

Geysers of shattered rock and earth began to blossom on the hills beyond. He could almost feel sorry for the bastards on the receiving end. Almost.

Beside him, Heywood had his eye to the rifle scope, watching the show. He certainly couldn't expect to find any targets in that carnage below. Nonetheless, Heywood nudged Pomeroy's arm.

"What?"

"Here, start spotting targets for me," the sniper said, pressing a pair of binoculars on Pomeroy.

"Spot your own damn targets."

"The lieutenant said—"

"Yeah, yeah. I heard what the lieutenant said. What I'd like to do with those binoculars is shove them sideways up your ass."

"Try it," Heywood said, taking his eye off the scope and giving Pomeroy his full attention. He was a big, muscular guy. Bigger than Pomeroy.

"Seriously? We are about to start an assault and you want to start a fight?"

On the other side of Pomeroy, the kid spoke up. "I'll take the binoculars," he said.

"Can you even see that far, Four Eyes?"

"I can see just fine with glasses on. Do you want a spotter or not?"

With a grunt of affirmation, the sniper handed them over. "Call out any targets you see and I'll eliminate them," he said.

The kid pushed his glasses up to fit the binoculars to his eyes. However, there was nothing to see except the airborne cloud of debris from the opposite hillside being churned by artillery bursts.

"Give 'em hell," Pomeroy muttered, dreading the moment that the shells stopped falling because that was when the attack would begin.

What Pomeroy and the rest of the troops poised to attack couldn't know was that the big guns were firing on mostly empty positions. Like the American troops, the Chinese had been on the move in the early morning pre-dawn. Unseen, they were now moving to flank the American position and launch a surprise attack. Planes didn't fly in the pre-dawn darkness, so without any air cover or reconnaissance, the American commanders were blind to the fact that they were about to be attacked by hundreds of enemy troops.

* * *

THE ARTILLERY HALTED FIRING ALL AT ONCE, like a summer downpour that stops as suddenly as it starts. But Pomeroy knew there weren't going to be any rainbows this morning.

"Get ready, fellas," he said, tensing himself to scramble over the top of the ridge and down the other side, then climb the opposite ridge toward the enemy troops waiting for them. Minutes went by, but the order never came. "What's the holdup?"

He knew that every moment that passed enabled the enemy to regroup after the bombardment and prepare for the attack.

Sure enough, they began to see Chinese soldiers in the distance, but well within rifle range. Uneasily, he recognized the fact that if he could see the Chinese, then they could see *him*. Pomeroy was itching to shoot, but knew that he had to await orders.

A few scattered enemy rifle shots began to pepper the American position.

"Target!" the sniper called. "I need a target."

"Uh, ten o'clock. There's a ditch with three or four Chinese in it."

Heywood shifted slightly. "I see it," he said.

Moments later, he fired.

"I think you missed," the kid said, his eyes pressed to the binoculars, glasses pushed up on his forehead.

"It's not my fault," Heywood said. "You need to do a better job of choosing targets."

"OK, those guys are still in the ditch."

Heywood shut up long enough to fire again. "Got 'em!" he said triumphantly.

"No ... I don't think so," the kid said, eyes still tight against the binoculars.

"Just for the record, you are doing one hell of a lousy job," Heywood complained. He shifted his bulk higher, hoping for a better vantage point.

More enemy fire was now finding targets. One thing about the Chinese was that their aim sure had improved, Pomeroy thought. They were not to be underestimated, which was what the American and U.N. forces had learned the hard way back at the Chosin Reservoir campaign. They were learning that lesson all over again at Triangle Hill.

A soldier a few feet to their left dropped stone dead, shot through the head.

"Better stay down," Pomeroy warned the sniper, who had stuck his head up above the rocks to get a better look at the enemy.

"I need to move forward to get a better shot," Heywood announced. "Spotter, you stay with me."

"Kid, you stay right where you are. It's suicide."

"I said—"

Heywood never had a chance to finish. A bullet hit him square in the chest and he slumped over.

"Aw, geez," the kid said, rolling Heywood over. He had one of those ugly, sucking chest wounds. Pink froth bubbling at his lips.

He's a goner, Pomeroy thought.

The kid was pressing on the wound, trying to staunch the flow of blood, but it wasn't any use. It wasn't so much the blood coming out, as the blood staying in. Heywood was essentially drowning in his own blood.

His eyes widened in fear and pain. Pomeroy didn't much like Heywood, but that didn't mean he wanted to see him die. Hell, Heywood was on their side. But there wasn't a damn thing anybody could do for him.

Pomeroy leaned over and gripped the dying man's shoulder. "It's all right," he said. What he meant by that was, *it's all right to die.*

Heywood's eyes rolled back in his head and he started to writhe, desperate for breath. Pomeroy held onto the man's shoulder, just to let him know that he wasn't alone. Then Heywood finally lay still.

Pomeroy looked up and locked eyes with the kid. The lenses of the kid's glasses were flecked with Heywood's blood. The eyes behind the glasses were wide with fright.

"Keep your head down and you'll be OK," Pomeroy said, trying to reassure him.

He looked over at Heywood's body. In death, the man looked like a sack of potatoes. Some sniper he had turned out to be.

Where the hell was Cole when you needed him?

That's when they heard the sound of bugles and whistles coming from their flanks. He had heard those same sounds more than a few times before, and the odd cacophony struck fear into his heart. With a shock, Pomeroy realized that while the Americans had been focused on attacking the Chinese positions directly in front of them, the enemy had somehow turned the tables and attacked them. A few bugles even sounded as if they were coming from behind them.

Sweet Jesus, have the Chinese surrounded us?

A pang of sheer terror stabbed through him, fearing that it was going to be like the standoff at Chosin all over again.

CHAPTER NINE

DEEP IN THE NIGHT, Chen awoke with the other troops and ate a simple breakfast of hot rice into which a raw egg had been cracked and stirred, creating a nourishing, creamy dish. This was washed down with plenty of piping, hot tea. Such rich food was indeed unusual and along with the early hour could mean just one thing. He and the others were being fed well in preparation for battle.

Normally, there was some intimation of such things that the long-time campaigners about them could sense in the way that the pain in an old man's knee warns that rain is coming. Chen had not sensed any of that, but the battle plan might simply have meant that a sudden opportunity had presented itself. They might even be reacting to some movement on the enemy's part. As a wise general once said, *Opportunities multiply as they are seized.*

He would not mind bringing the fight to the Americans and their U.N. allies once again. With their well-supplied troops and warplanes, along with their Caucasian skins, the enemy seemed to believe in their own superiority. But time and again, Chen and his rifle had taught them otherwise. He existed to punish the enemy. For that reason, if for no other, Chen welcomed the promise of the coming dawn.

Chen looked around at the growing light, trying to get a sense of what the day would bring. He could see groups of officers moving around, including the dreaded commissars talking among themselves as if they harbored some secret. That in itself was not unusual, but this morning, there seemed to be actual plans afoot.

Studying the political officers in their fine uniforms, so much better than those worn by the rank-and-file soldiers, Chen thought, *We are all just peasants to them.*

Chen considered that the revolution was supposed to mean something. It was what he and so many others had fought for, but he saw now that he had been naive.

The revolution was meant to transform their society, but in the end nothing had changed. He would always be one of the peasants, even as a designated sniper.

Chen's duties were separated from those of the regular soldiers. Once he had finished breakfast, he began gathering his equipment. Russian rifle with telescopic sight. Ammunition. Canteen and a cold, boiled yam that he slipped into a pocket. A highly coveted pair of binoculars that he kept in a day pack, out of sight until he reached the place where he would work that day. Like a peasant going into the fields, he thought, except that instead of harvesting crops, he would be harvesting the lives of enemy soldiers.

Punishing them for their arrogance.

His plan was to move into position on one of the ridges that overlooked the American forces and harass them during the day. If he was lucky, he might even be able to target a few of their officers.

Chen hated the Americans deeply. He sensed their overconfidence. He sensed that they thought so little of the Chinese and looked down upon them. They had dared to invade the Korean peninsula and had threatened China itself for that. They were now paying the price.

Chen himself had exacted a heavy toll against the American and UN forces. He had lost count of how many soldiers he had shot, but Major Wu informed him that it was more than one hundred. Chen wasn't sure about that. The number may have been greater or lower than that, but he was wise enough to know that whatever Major Wu reported was the correct number.

As if summoned by Chen's thoughts, he saw Major Wu

approaching him. Now Wu had traded his dress coat that he normally wore for a simple field jacket. His fancy officer's cap had been replaced by a fur-trimmed *Ushanka* that was ubiquitous among the Chinese troops. The hats were warm and practical as cold weather arrived in the mountains. Officially, the hats were trimmed in wolf fur, but Chen suspected that it was dog fur. No matter. The hats kept them warm all the same.

"There you are," Wu said happily, upon seeing Chen. "I've been looking for you."

"Yes, sir," Chen said, feeling himself instantly on guard. Having Wu looking for you could never be a good thing. Of course, it was Wu who had brought him to this battlefield. Wu never did anything without purpose. It was Wu's hope to use Chen to help put pressure on the Americans. It was one thing for the Americans to see their boys killed by bombs and bullets, but there was something horrifying about the thought of them being singled out and killed by a sniper. Wu had explained to Chen that such things helped to turn the Americans back home away from the war in distaste, because they had no stomach for that sort of war.

"You and I have work to do today," the major said cheerfully.

"Yes, sir."

Chen nodded, managing to keep his face a mask. Simply put, work meant killing. He did not share the major's cheerfulness. While he was as eager as anyone to punish the Americans, it was serious business.

"You don't say much, do you, Chen? No matter. Whenever there is something to say that matters, I shall say it for you."

Chen preferred working alone, but he saw now that Major Wu carried a set of binoculars and also a rifle, which was uncharacteristic for the commissar.

"Of course, sir," Chen said. "I will do as you direct me."

"Good, good," Wu said. "We are going to head up into the hills and provide support for the attack."

"The attack, sir?"

"Yes, yes. The attack. The Americans are launching an attack of their own this morning."

"How do we know, sir?"

"We have our spies, just as they do, Chen. We are going to let them come and think that they have pushed us off the ridge that they so desperately want. Meanwhile, we will have moved around to their flank. We may even be able to get some troops to attack them from the rear if we can maintain the element of surprise."

Chen understood now the activity this morning and the hearty breakfast. He could see the officers organizing the troops, forming up the squads and companies in what looked like marching order. Although there were veterans such as Chen among the ranks, most of the Chinese troops were conscripts with very little training. They caught on quickly, but any large-scale action generated its share of confusion. At least now, the Chinese army had resolved its issue with not being able to equip every soldier with a rifle.

When the Chinese had first crossed the Yalu River last autumn in support of North Korea, there were rifles for only about half the men. Those in the first ranks of attackers were armed. The second wave of attackers carried hand grenades—or simply waited for someone with a rifle to fall. Most of the new weapons had come from their communist comrades in the Soviet Union or had been captured from U.N. forces.

Chen was no general, but even he could see the brilliance of the plan that Wu had just outlined. The Americans were always so convinced of their superiority that they would keep advancing into the hills, certain that their enemy had fled and that they had won the day. The Americans were always so certain of victory that they were blind to the possibility of anything else.

Meanwhile, they were being outsmarted. It was as if the Americans and their allies were dogs and the Chinese forces were like the foxes of the Mongol plains, ever more agile and cunning.

Chen smiled at the thought.

Major Wu smiled back. "Good. I can see that you approve of the plan. Let's go."

"Yes, sir."

They moved through the camp and Chen inhaled the smells of cooking fires and hot tea and food. Comforting smells for a soldier and not so different from mornings on a farm or in the small villages that most of the soldiers had come from. What was lacking this morning, however, were the usual jokes and laughter. Instead, an air of deadly seriousness and intent had settled over the Chinese camp. There was a realization that many who went into action this morning likely would not return.

Chen led the way over the familiar ground and Wu followed. Chen had taken this path many times before, winding his way up into the ridges facing the American defenses.

He climbed higher and higher, his legs easily covering the steep ground. He came to a place where the path had washed out in the last heavy rain and had to jump nearly a meter across the gully. The ground rose steeply on the other side. Major Wu struggled to keep up, huffing and puffing. Chen's nimble feet picked a way across the rocky ground. Once or twice, Wu slipped and fell, leaving his pristine uniform streaked with mud.

"Should we rest, sir?" Chen asked the next time that Wu fell, making sure to keep his face turned away so that Wu didn't see his grin.

"Yes, yes, just for a moment," Wu said. He tipped up his canteen and took a drink, then offered it to Chen.

Chen took a drink, anticipating a few sips of cool water, and gagged at the alcohol that ran down his throat. "Rice wine?"

"We must fortify ourselves, Chen," the major explained. "Besides, most of the water here would make you ill. It is unhealthy. Better to drink rice wine!"

It was true that many men had been affected with runny bowels due to the bad water, which was why it was mostly boiled now to make tea. However, it would only be someone like Wu who could fill his canteen with rice wine. Better prepared now, Chen took a long drink and enjoyed the feeling of warmth that spread through him in the morning chill.

"Much better, sir," Chen said, handing back the canteen.

"Do well today, Chen, and I will see to it that you get your own rice wine. Maybe a whole bottle."

Now that Wu had caught his breath, they pressed on, finally reaching a point where the forward sentries were located. They nodded at Chen in recognition because he had visited here before. His

Russian sniper rifle with its telescopic sight was instantly recognizable.

He and Wu were now slightly above the opposing ridge where the Americans were present in strength. He could see them lined up along the ridge in the early morning half-light.

"Look at them all," Wu said. "There won't be nearly that many returning when this morning's work is finished. With luck, they will retreat right into our own bayonets behind them!"

Major Wu spoke with a certainty that Chen himself did not feel. In the past, he had seen how the Chinese paid a heavy price against the superior weapons of the enemy. Of course, it was doubt and fear that kept a soldier alive. Wisely, he did not share his misgivings with the political officer.

Pushing doubt from his mind, Chen focused on his work. There were several places already along the ridge where he had plied his trade as a sniper.

He knew that it went against several tenets of the sniper rulebook to shoot from the same position on more than one day, but he had moved around enough that he felt confident. No one would know where to expect him next. Besides, in his experience so far, he did not have an equal among the Americans. It was true that they had a sniper or two firing from their own position, but so far, their efforts had not been able to displace or even threaten Chen. *They are the dogs*, he reminded himself. *I am the fox.*

He was now located directly across from the ridge where two rocky outcroppings rose up. He thought they looked like the ears of a cat. The rocky protuberances on the ridge line created a distinctive landmark. He set his rifle across a stone and peered through the scope, ready to get down to business. He put a rag under the stock to cushion the weapon. The barrel itself was already wrapped in scraps of cloth in order to help break up the outline of the rifle and better disguise it from enemy eyes.

"When the Americans attack, thin them out as much as you can," Wu said. "We don't want to make this too easy for them. Remember, the bulk of our men will move around their flank and attack their rear."

Chen nodded, not bothering to speak, already slipping into his role as a sniper. *Let them come*, he thought. *I will strike like the eagle from above.*

Predictably, the American artillery began to fire, the shells falling into the camp that they had vacated just a short time ago. Most of the troops were already gone, rushing to flank the American defenses and drive a sword into their rear support areas. Of course, the American gunners would think that they were wreaking destruction on the enemy.

"Look at that," Major Wu said approvingly, watching the geysers of earth erupting on the hillside below. "Their shells fall on nothing."

Calling the targeted area *nothing* wasn't entirely accurate—a few soldiers had been left behind to guard the encampment. Many wounded were also in that encampment, now bearing the brunt of the bombardment. No matter, Chen thought. The ruse had worked.

Through the rifle scope, he began to pick out targets. There were so many. He did not simply shoot the first man whom his sights touched. He wanted to pick out the richest targets. An officer or a radio operator. In part, this was why Wu had come along. With the binoculars, he was able to see a much broader picture of the ridge where the Americans crouched, awaiting their order to advance.

Wu made an approving grunt. He had spotted a suitable target. The political officer knew his business, at least. "I think I see an enemy sniper," he said, and directed Chen's view that way.

Through the scope, the target sprang closer. Chen could see him now, an American soldier with a rifle that had a telescopic sight. The American snipers were few and far between, and briefly, he wondered if this was the same sniper that he had encountered back at the Chosin Reservoir. He remembered that man well because the sniper's cold eyes still haunted him. In some ways, it had been like looking into a mirror.

The enemy soldier had only escaped in the end because he had tricked Chen with a decoy. The decoy—the corpse of one of his fellow soldiers—had been rigged with a grenade that had killed two of the men accompanying Chen. Chen himself had only narrowly escaped. By then, the American sniper had gotten away. Could this possibly be the same man? Chen had no real way of knowing at this distance.

The enemy's rifle stood out because he had not bothered to camouflage it in any way. This sniper did not seem particularly concerned with keeping himself hidden. Like so many of his comrades, perhaps he thought that he was invincible.

He watched the man move forward on the ridge, leaving himself even more exposed. A few Chinese troops below were firing at the American position, mainly to hold their attention as the main body of Chinese slipped away. The sniper seemed intent on trying to pick off some of these men.

Chen put the sights on the enemy sniper and slowly began to squeeze the trigger.

"That's it," Wu said gleefully, nearly into Chen's ear. "You've got him."

Chen ignored the annoying political officer and shut out everything but the target visible in his rifle scope. Slowly, slowly, he took up tension on the trigger. The distance was at the limits of what he could accurately hit, and the slightest miscalculation would send the bullet astray.

Finally, the rifle kicked against his shoulder.

"We got him!" Wu whispered.

The major spoke as if it had been his eye looking through the sight and pulling the trigger. Chen looked through the scope, seeing that the body of the sniper was indeed now slumped in the rock and dirt. The sniper had a spotter, and Chen worked the bolt, thinking that he might shoot this soldier as well, but the spotter scurried back under cover before Chen could get his sights on him.

"Congratulations on your fine work as a spotter, sir," Chen said, carefully keeping the slightest trace of sarcasm from his voice.

"Yes, yes, thank you," Wu agreed, sounding pleased. The binoculars were pressed against his eyes as he scanned the ridge. "Who else can we shoot? Fortunately for us, we have an entire ridge filled with targets."

For once, Chen thought, he and Wu had something that they could agree upon.

CHAPTER TEN

PARING KNIFE IN HAND, Cole studied the potato that he held. It was just as unremarkable as the hundreds of other potatoes that had passed through his hands recently. *Reckon I'd be happy if I don't never see another spud again so long as I live.* Leastways, not a potato on the wrong side of his plate.

But that was kitchen duty for you, so he didn't have much room to complain. This is what he had asked for, in a way, to be sequestered from the fighting, to not be carrying a rifle, to just bide his time until he could go home again to the mountains.

If that meant peeling an actual mountain of potatoes to get there, that would be just fine with him.

Or was it? Deep down, Cole knew that him being here in the kitchen was like sending a tiger to catch a mouse. Mostly, he was worried about Pomeroy and the kid. Pomeroy could handle himself, but Cole knew that the man was hiding the fact that he was still hurting after the Chosin Reservoir. Pomeroy was no better than an old jalopy with a new coat of paint. As for the kid, he had a lot of spirit, but he needed someone to be there watching his back.

He thought about the kid writing a letter home and hoped to hell that it wouldn't be the last one that the kid wrote. He would have been part of the assault force that had moved out before dawn. They'd be getting into it soon, Cole knew, because now they could hear the artillery softening up the enemy positions.

It ought to be me going out there, Cole thought, reaching for another spud. *Instead, here I am, peeling potatoes.*

Since the incident with Tater, everyone pretty much let him alone in the kitchen. Settling that bully's hash had not made him into a mess-tent hero—not that this was the reason Cole had beaten the man down. Besides, Cole didn't have any regrets. The man had it coming.

However, the incident had left the other kitchen staff more than a little fearful of him. Somewhere along the line, word had gotten out that Cole was in the Army to avoid prison for killing two men. Maybe he had Tommy Wilson to thank for letting that little gem slip? No matter—if the rest of the kitchen staff left him alone, so much the better.

Slowly, Cole was working his way through that huge pile of potatoes. He wouldn't even think about all the pots he would have to scrub later. His rough hands were even more raw and red.

This was more than enough to keep him busy for now. He had gotten all the scut jobs, that was for certain sure.

In some ways, a battlefield commander could learn a few lessons from the mess tent cooks. Men ran back and forth, carrying trays and kettles brimming with soup, scalding hot pots of coffee, and stacks of dirty dishes and utensils. The scene was chaotic, and yet somehow everything ran just fine, with soldiers dodging around one another without colliding or spilling a drop.

"Make way!" someone shouted, lugging an oversized pot. "Coming through!" The busy staff parted before him like the Red Sea had made way for Moses.

Cole shook his head, impressed. He had seen less action on a few battlefields than in this kitchen, and that was a fact.

His thoughts were interrupted by an odd popping sound. He looked up to see that a big glass jug of vinegar on a shelf near his head had shattered, spewing its contents everywhere. That was remarkable enough, until a Number 10 can of green beans sitting on the same shelf suddenly sprang a hole and began spouting bean juice across the broken glass and scattered vinegar. It was the damnedest thing. Mighty strange.

Cole had no idea what was going on, other than that there was now a bigger mess to clean up. He turned back to his potatoes.

But then, one of the soldiers carrying a big tray cried out sharply in pain and dropped the tray, before following it to the floor himself.

The kitchen workers saw what was going on, but barely stopped what they were doing, no more than momentarily sidetracked as they rushed through their duties. Another can on the shelf sprang a leak. A soldier stumbled and fell as he was carrying a pot. He didn't get back up, but lay still in a puddle of soup.

What the hell?

Then Cole figured it out. They were taking fire. Bullets zipped through the kitchen, but the rifle fire was so far away, and the clatter of the kitchen and cooking food was so loud, that they couldn't hear the actual gunshots in the distance. Still, there was no doubt that they were under fire. Cole got down on the floor with all those potato peelings.

That's when a soldier came running in from the mess hall.

"We're under attack!" he shouted. "The Chinese are coming down out of the hills like goddamn locusts."

Having delivered his message, the soldier spun on his heels and ran out.

Most of the men in the mess tent were not combat effectives and had not seen much in the way of action—at least as much as that was possible in a war zone. They didn't really know what to do.

For his own part, Cole was glad to be done with those goddamn potatoes. He tossed aside his paring knife.

"Get down!" he yelled at the others as more cans sprang leaks and jars shattered. Hit by a bullet, a big cast-iron frying pan hanging over a stove rang like a gong. "Best grab your rifles, boys, unless you plan on inviting them Chinese to supper."

Taking his own advice, Cole began crawling on his hands and knees between the tables and racks, making his way toward the door.

For a while now, Cole had been carrying his rifle into the mess hall, although most of the others didn't bother to do that anymore, although it was part of regulations in a combat zone. This morning's incursion by the Chinese was a case in point. How did the others plan to fight them off—maybe with a ladle?

Cole ripped off his white mess hat along with his apron, grabbed his rifle from where he had left it near the doorway, and ran out into a world of chaos.

It wasn't full daylight yet, so the surroundings were murky, but flares lit the sky. Fired by the Chinese, the slow-burning flares overhead turned the gray dawn into day, as if lightning had frozen in the sky to reveal the surrounding hills. The pale, flickering light illuminated a nightmarish scene of confused soldiers running in every direction.

Adding to the chaotic scene, Cole heard trumpets, bugles, banging drums, and whistles. These alien sounds provoked fear and confusion among the Americans. In the distance, he could see lines of enemy troops streaming down from the hills. It was the Chosin Reservoir all over again. He could scarcely believe his own eyes. Was this really happening?

The Chinese forces drove like a spear point into the flank of the forces on the ridge and into the rear encampment as well. The entire camp had been thrown into chaos by the attack that had come without warning. Most of the combat troops were on the nearest ridge, ready to launch an attack. Support troops scurried everywhere, almost like ants.

Everywhere he looked in the blazing light, American positions were a jumble of confusion. A few officers and sergeants shouted and ran around trying to organize a defense, but Cole had his own plan in mind. Ignoring them, Cole ran on alone, thinking that he just wanted to find Pomeroy and the kid, Tommy Wilson. There was a chance that he could help them and in a mess like this, you needed your friends watching your back. They would need him, and so would the entire squad if it was coming up against an attack.

The question was, where were they? Somewhere on the ridge ahead.

He grabbed a company clerk who was running past—away from the Chinese, Cole noticed. Then again, it was his experience that when men were running away, it was usually for a good reason. "Where's Fox Company at?"

"Over there on the ridge," the clerk said. "Trying to hold back the Chinese. God help 'em."

Cole let the man go and ran in that direction. Sniper Ridge was just beyond HQ and the unit had been up there before. If nothing else, he would add his rifle to help the poor bastards who were trying to defend that position right now in the frenzied semi-darkness.

It was hard to tell who was friend and who was foe. The ghostly, quilted uniforms of the Chinese soldiers were well-suited to the gloaming and hid them well. Only at the last instant did the defenders see them as they surged out of the pre-dawn darkness.

Another clue was that most of the enemy was shouting insanely in a language that Cole couldn't even begin to understand. Sounded like gibberish to him.

Two Chinese charged at him out of the darkness. Cole simply leveled his rifle at them and pulled the trigger without even aiming, dropping first one man and then the other. He went to one knee, scanning the darkness and sure enough, two more Chinese came out of nowhere. Cole fired twice and these other enemy soldiers met the same fate.

He got up and ran on, heading for the ridge. All around him, he could hear more bugles and shouts, along with the staccato crackle of small arms fire. Tracer rounds stitched the gloom, creating a crazy quilt of fire coming down from the nearest hills. If it hadn't been so terrifying, it might have been beautiful, like some fascinating Fourth of July fireworks show, but there was no time to stand still and watch. The red tracers erupted across the level plain that held the encampment. It was a wonder that he hadn't been hit.

Cole jumped over a body, realizing it was a dead American in a white apron. Some poor bastard from the mess tent had bought it. The Chinese attack was having deadly consequences.

He had to keep going. More Chinese surged in his direction and Cole emptied the M1 at them, then jumped down into a foxhole so that he could reload without being exposed. The enemy troops rushed by, not noticing him in the murkiness of the early morning light.

As he held his breath, Cole quickly realized that he was not alone in the bottom of the foxhole. Someone else was there. It was a strange thing, but he could actually *smell* that it wasn't an American. The cowering body next to him reeked of garlic or onions. Definitely not hamburgers and fried potatoes and cigarettes, which was the aroma that usually hung about American troops. No, this was a Chinese stink.

In the light from an overhead flare, Cole could see a terrified round face next to him, eyes wide as saucers. The man did not even seem to have a rifle, but only stared at Cole, mumbling something that might have been a prayer. Maybe the poor bastard was just trying to surrender. If the enemy soldier had been of a mind to, he could have shot or bayoneted Cole as soon as he jumped into the hole.

Grateful that he was still breathing, Cole didn't want this frightened soldier to start shouting and alert the large number of Chinese troops running past Cole.

Cole put his finger to his lips in the universal gesture for silence, all the while keeping his rifle aimed in the enemy soldier's direction. The man saw Cole's gesture and nodded furiously.

Cole finished reloading his rifle, stuck his head above the rim of the hole to make sure there weren't any Chinese in the vicinity, and then crawled out and started running again toward the ridge.

It was fine by him if that Chinese fella in the foxhole wanted to sit this fight out. Good luck to him.

Now, the attackers had brought a few mortars into play and the shells fell among the tents and trucks, adding to the chaos. Metal splinters whistled through the air. Cole kept running, away from the chaos behind him and toward the ridge ahead.

On the American side, the artillery was still raining shells on the Chinese lines, cloaking the sounds of the Chinese attack on the rear. How the artillery could tell what they were firing at, Cole had no idea. However, it had been his experience that artillery fire didn't need to be all that accurate. Nobody was going to mistake one of those big guns for a sniper rifle anytime soon.

He ran forward, keeping low, not completely sure who was nearby in the darkness. The whole damn situation was crazy. If he had any sense, he'd go and run in the other direction. He reckoned, though, that there wasn't any safe place to go. Not with the Chinese swarming in the dawn. Cole ran on, leaping a low wall of sandbags, then dodging a fresh mortar crater.

He finally reached the ridge with its defensive line, where men were firing in the general direction of the Chinese, not even aware of the attack on the rear. It was hard to say if the shooting was doing any good. Cole ran down the line, recognizing a few of the other soldiers. Finally, he saw Pomeroy and the kid next to each other behind a pile of rocks. Both of them looked up in surprise when Cole slid into position next to them.

"Where the hell have you been?" Pomeroy asked.

"Peeling potatoes," Cole said. "Thought I'd take a break."

"Well, it's about time you showed up. Glad you're here. We saved some of these Chinese for you."

"I'll see what I can do," Cole said.

He looked out at the grayness ahead of them, noticing that the landscape seemed to shift like something fluid, and realized he wasn't looking at rocks and hills, but at an oncoming line of enemy troops. Unless they got lucky, in the next few minutes the American line was about to be overrun.

Cole fired the rifle until the action locked open. That was all the ammo that he had. He wished that he still had his old Springfield. A thought occurred to him. "Where the hell is your fancy new sniper, anyhow?"

"Dead," Pomeroy said, nodding toward the body located several feet forward of the squad's position. "He got himself plugged right off the bat. Looks like he tangled with a Chinese sniper."

"Goddamn idiot," Cole said. "There's no cover there. What was he thinking?"

"Worst of it is that he almost got the kid killed, too. The kid was spotting for him."

Cole looked over at the kid, who, despite the terror evident on his face, was still managing to fire at the oncoming enemy troops.

"I want his rifle," Cole said, then corrected himself. "*My* rifle."

"You can't go out there. It's suicide."

"Right now, being on this whole dang ridge is suicide," Cole said. "Cover me."

He crouched and ran toward Heywood's body. With professional interest, he noted that the bullet had struck Heywood square in the front of his helmet. Cole could see the man's eyes staring. Unless that had been a lucky shot, the Chinese sniper opposite them was awfully good.

Keeping that in mind, Cole threw himself flat on the rock, willing his belly to sink into the stone. He kept Heywood's body in front of him, using it like a sandbag. A bullet *thwacked* into the corpse. That was no stray bullet. The Chinese sniper was still out there, and he had definitely seen Cole.

Cole reached out and got a grip on the rifle strap, but there was a problem. The rifle wouldn't come free, having been partially pinned under Heywood's dead weight. Cole tugged harder, which jiggled Heywood's body. *Thwack*, went another bullet.

Cole slid forward, keeping himself as low as possible. The rim of his helmet grated against the rock, but he didn't dare take it off right now.

He let go of the strap and got a better grasp on the rifle stock itself. His hands moved over the familiar wood and got a good grip. He bunched the strength in his upper arms and shoulders, preparing to give a mighty tug to free the rifle, but to his surprise, the rifle slid free as smoothly as a sword from a scabbard.

He and Old Betsy were back in business.

Heywood had extra clips stuffed into his pockets, and Cole fished those out.

He peered back over his shoulder at the several feet of bare, rock ledge that he would need to cross to rejoin the rest of the squad. Wasn't gonna happen, not with that sniper on him like a fly on horse manure. He'd only managed to get out here in the first place because the sniper's attention must have been elsewhere. Now, that sniper would be waiting for his next move. He'd have to shoot his way out.

Slowly, he eased the rifle across Heywood's body. At least the dead man was proving useful, after all. He sure as hell hadn't lasted long as a sniper.

The daylight was growing fast toward an overcast autumn day, but the dim light was alive with muzzle flashes and tracer fire. This was a distraction, but Cole's practiced eye knew just what it was looking for.

There. Just as another bullet struck the corpse, Cole spotted a muzzle flash just about where he expected the Chinese sniper to be lurking. Keeping the sight picture of where he had seen that flash, he fired back.

Then came another muzzle flash. Another bullet hit Heywood's body.

He worked the bolt, fired again just where he had seen that flash.

* * *

FROM THE CHINESE SIDE, Chen watched the battle unfold. It was clear that the Americans had planned to launch an attack, but had not expected to be struck first by the Chinese. Yet more evidence, he thought, that the Americans were overconfident fools.

"There, on your right. I think it is an American officer," Wu said helpfully, binoculars pressed tight to his eyes.

Chen grunted in reply. He was sure that in Wu's report, every man that Chen shot would be an officer. Under Wu's helpful supervision, of course.

He pulled the trigger. The man went down.

Then something else caught Chen's eye. He saw a man break away from the main line of defense and dart a few feet forward, too fast for Chen to get a shot at him. Scurrying like a true American rat. To his surprise, this rat had run right to where the American sniper had fallen.

"Did you see that?" the sharp-eyed Wu said. Chen was impressed; Wu was starting to catch on to this sniping business. "He's up to something."

"I saw him," Chen said. It was likely that the man had run out to retrieve the dead man's sniper rifle. He tried to pick the soldier off, but he was taking cover behind his dead comrade. Chen fired anyhow, hitting the corpse, giving the man something to think about.

"You missed," Wu said.

Chen ignored him. Instead, he kept his eye tight against the scope, focused on the ridge below, hoping that the man would raise his head just enough to give Chen a target.

The man below chanced a look, raising his head sufficiently for Chen to glimpse the symbol painted on the front of his helmet. With a jolt, he realized that he had seen this symbol before. The American sniper from the Chosin Reservoir had a similar flag on his helmet.

Wu had seen it, too. "What's he got on his helmet? I don't recognize that insignia."

"It is a flag," Chen said.

"Shoot him!"

Before he could fire, the man had ducked his head. Again, Chen fired anyway.

He felt a whisper of uneasiness. In all the months since the Chosin Reservoir, he had not seen any other soldiers with that symbol. Could this be the same man that he had confronted at the Chosin Reservoir? He must be a marksman; why else would he have made an effort to retrieve the dead sniper's rifle?

As if in answer to Chen's question, a bullet came in, whipping past off to his left. The American must be shooting at him. However, there was almost nothing to see, no target for him to aim at. Instead, he fired again into the corpse, hoping to rattle the marksman.

For his trouble, a bullet struck inches from where Chen hid, stinging his face with particles of rock and dirt. The bullet made a *twang* sound as it ricocheted off the stone ledge. He glanced over at Major Wu, who was wide-eyed with surprise. The zip of bullets overhead was one thing, but there was something about the sound of a ricochet that was enough to shiver anyone's spine.

The American sniper must have zeroed in on his muzzle flash. It was time to go.

"We have to move," he said to Wu.

For once, the political officer didn't seem to mind taking an order.

* * *

Without waiting to see if the enemy sniper would shoot back, Cole slithered backward across the rock. Hopefully, he had at least convinced the son of a bitch to duck. Cole scooted back, half-expecting to get shot in the head at any moment.

Something pounded him in the hip, but he kept going. His side grew wet.

Once he got closer to the squad's position, he felt two pairs of strong hands grab him by the ankles and start to pull him back. He didn't resist as he was hauled into the foxhole. He lay in the bottom, panting.

"Am I hit? Am I hit?" Oddly, he didn't feel any pain.

Pomeroy patted him down, looking him over. "I think you're still in one piece."

"Goddamn."

He suddenly felt desperately thirsty, and Cole reached for his canteen. There was nothing in it. There was now a large bullet hole in his canteen, which explained why he had felt something strike his hip, along with the wetness. Another couple of inches and the sniper's bullet would have shattered his hip.

Pomeroy noticed the damaged canteen. "That was close."

"Somebody give me their canteen, dammit." The kid handed his over, and Cole gulped the water down greedily

He noticed the reporter nearby, cradling the camera in his hands. Bullets zipped overhead, but he seemed intent only on taking pictures. Cole reckoned the reporter was either dedicated, or a dang fool. He'd had a weapon slung over his shoulder before, but now it was nowhere to be seen.

"Get down," Cole snapped at him.

"That was amazing!"

The reporter started to level his camera at Cole.

"Hold on, boy. Take my picture and I'll shoot your ass."

Pomeroy recognized Cole's tone. "Better put that away. He's serious."

"All right. Sorry.

"Don't worry about shooting pictures right now. Shoot some Chinese. Where's your carbine?"

"Right there." The soldier had leaned it against the wall of the foxhole. *Dang fool*, Cole decided. *The Chinese are attacking and he's busy taking pictures.*

"Get your weapon and start pulling the trigger or the only thing you get in the paper will be your name on the casualties list."

Pomeroy was smirking at him. "You ready to go back to the mess tent yet?" he asked.

"To hell with that," Cole said, and reached for his rifle. "I've peeled enough potatoes to last me a lifetime."

CHAPTER ELEVEN

WHEN THE ORDER came to attack, there was no blowing of bugles or beating of drums, as there had been from the Chinese lines. The officers and sergeants simply shouted, "Let's go!" and waved their hands. With that, the American troops surged up and over the ridge.

Some poor bastards never made it more than a few feet before an enemy bullet cut them down.

Cole found himself screaming the same rebel yell that had echoed at Gettysburg and Antietam and a hundred other battlefields. Cole realized that he felt no fear. He felt *unleashed*.

Just like the Yankees who had heard that weird, high pitched yelping nearly a century ago, the Chinese who heard it now felt their bellies clench in fright. Something bad was coming for them. Maybe these Americans were not as soft as their leaders had told them.

Through the valley where they had driven back the earlier Chinese assault as dawn arrived, Cole, Pomeroy and the kid ran with the others, their rifles at the ready, but careful to be spread out so that a single burst of machine-gun fire or a mortar round wouldn't wipe them all out. Dimly, Cole was aware of the reporter somewhere off to his right, still wielding a camera instead of a rifle. *Dang fool.* He looked ahead.

Their objective was the top of a steep hill with the name of sniper ridge.

From behind them, they could also hear shooting as the soldiers in the encampment held back the Chinese attack in the rear area. The American assault on Sniper Ridge would bring the attack to the enemy.

They were close enough now that he could see some of the Chinese defenders up there. From the looks of it, they were spread too thin, which was a good thing. The bad thing was that the American attackers would have to scramble to climb this steep ridge.

He reckoned that somewhere up on that ridge was the Chinese sniper that he had taken a pot shot at this morning. Unless Cole had gotten lucky and settled his hash, this same sniper would be shooting at them again soon enough.

"Keep it moving, keep it moving!" Lieutenant Ballard was shouting, leading the way. If Cole had his rebel yell, all that Ballard needed was a sword to play the part of an old-time infantry officer.

Cole had to give the lieutenant at least some credit. He didn't much like Ballard. Hell, the feeling was mutual, because Ballard had made it clear that he didn't much like Cole.

On the battlefield, those issues melted away. They attacked the enemy as one. He had the lieutenant's back, and the lieutenant had his.

The lieutenant was right out in front of his men. It took some brass to do that, Cole decided. Meanwhile, the Chinese weren't simply going to let them stroll up the hill. From the heights of Sniper Ridge, the enemy began to pour fire down on the advancing American troops. It was light enough now that there was no predawn twilight to screen them from the enemy guns. They were crossing a no-man's land filled with shell holes, rocks, and bodies. If it wasn't exactly hell itself, then it was at least hell's front porch.

Walls of tangled concertina wire impeded their progress. Some men had brought along wire cutters and were hacking away now at the coiled strands, but it was taking too damn long, holding up the attack. The advancing line was out in the open and made an easy target for the Chinese defenders.

"We're pinned down," Cole said. "Gonna be hell to pay."

* * *

WHEN THE ATTACK BEGAN, Don Hardy ran with the others, stumbling over rocks and shattered tree stumps. There was no time to think, but only to act.

He didn't get far. His boot caught on something and he went flying, but struggled to keep the precious camera from smashing into the ground. Instead, he ended up sprawled face-down in the dirt. His breath went out of him with an *oopf* sound and sensation that he remembered from his schoolyard football days. It was like he had just been tackled by Korea.

He was tempted to lay there and claim that he had twisted his ankle, but in the end, his conscious wouldn't let him. He hadn't signed on to be part of an infantry attack. Instead, he had pictured himself interviewing soldiers in the foxholes, before heading back to the mess tent for a hot cup of coffee.

There was no time to whine about the situation in which he had found himself and there was nobody to listen, anyhow. He forced himself to his knees. As soon as he tried to get up and run, he saw that the attack was moving so quickly that he was already some distance behind the others. *Some reporter you are*, he thought. *You're letting the story get away from you.*

Back on his feet, he sprinted after the other soldiers to keep up, the carbine bouncing on his shoulder. He was more intent on observing the battle and shooting pictures than on shooting his weapon.

He cradled his precious camera in his hands, realizing that he was too worried about taking a few pictures to even be afraid. He wondered if something was wrong with him for thinking that. He was only dimly aware of the battle sounds around him: chattering machine guns, the *pop, pop, pop* of rifle fire. Dimly, he reminded himself that these were details that could go into one of his dispatches from the front.

He spotted a few men he recognized up ahead and decided to stick with the squad that he had found himself with earlier. That squad had included the hillbilly sniper. At least, that was how Hardy thought of him. He saw the man raise his rifle to fire, and Hardy snapped a photograph.

Something about the sniper was reassuring, simply because he seemed like one tough customer. If anybody was going to survive this attack, it was probably going to be somebody like that hillbilly. It came to Hardy in a flash that this was the same man with the Confederate flag on his helmet that he had seen when the Jeep carrying him into the camp had arrived.

Wait for me, he thought.

Hardy shadowed Cole and the two other squad members that he seemed to hang around with. A part of him registered that the most terrifying aspect of combat was the noise. Bullets whistled overhead and mortar rounds exploded, spewing rock and dirt into the air. He could hear men screaming battle cries as they ran up on the steep ridge where Chinese guns blazed down at the Americans. He could see the muzzle flashes in the distance like little firecrackers going off on the Fourth of July. But those flashes were far deadlier than a few firecrackers. All around him, men stumbled and fell, never to rise again. Although his mind dimly registered that these men were dead, Hardy had no choice but to keep running and keep up with the squad. When the soldiers ahead of him threw themselves down, he did the same and got his camera up long enough to shoot a few photographs of the assault.

He took another photo of the sniper at work and hoped that his hands weren't shaking so much that the photograph would be too blurry. Then the sniper and the others got up and ran on. Hardy launched himself after them, running pell-mell toward the ridge with the others.

The assault on the ridge seemed impossible. The ground was too steep. There were too many defenders and their bullets filled the air.

Hardy was fairly certain that he was going to die.

His heart hammered in his chest. His ears rang from the concussions. Color seemed to have leached out of the world, like a faded film.

There was nothing glorious here. It certainly wasn't like Lord Tennyson's poem about the Light Brigade riding to death and glory. There was only dirt and smoke and gore on the ground, and the screams of the wounded and the terrified attackers. Hardy gripped his camera for dear life, like a talisman, remembering to snap a few photos whenever the assault paused. He realized, though, that he kept forgetting to use his thumb to wind the roll, thus shooting one exposure on top of another.

Hardy took a deep breath and forced his shaking hands to advance the film.

* * *

COLE and the rest of the squad fired at the ridge, but they were stuck. If they didn't advance through the tangled obstacle created by the tangled wire, they were going to be caught out here in the open while the enemy cut them to pieces.

"This whole damn thing is getting bogged down," Pomeroy muttered, taking a knee next to Cole and watching for enemy targets.

"Go across my back!" somebody shouted nearby.

To Cole's amazement, he watched as a soldier threw himself down on the barbed wire, creating a human bridge through the mess.

Normally, his comrades might have been shocked, but in this case, out of fear and with adrenaline pumping, they simply ran across his back, crushing him deeper into the barbs.

Somebody else got the same idea, but this time they took the corpse of a dead Chinese soldier and threw him across the wire. Then they added a couple more bodies and the wire was pressed down effectively enough to create a bridge across the barrier.

American soldiers began to pour across that bridge of corpses and swarm up the steep ridge ahead.

"Stick with me, kid," Cole urged Tommy Wilson, throwing himself down beside the kid as a burst from a machine gun chewed up the rocks and dirt.

"Can you see him?" Cole wondered, putting his rifle to his shoulder. "You point me in the right direction and I'll shoot him."

The problem was that for Cole to see any larger area of the ridge, now that they were so close, he would have to take his eye away from this telescopic sight. Using the kid's eyes instead would help him to stay focused on individual targets.

"There he is. Ten o'clock," the kid said.

Cole swung the muzzle and spotted the heads of the machine gunners trying to mow them down. He was fairly certain it was one of the Degtyaryov light machine guns provided to the Chinese courtesy of the USSR. He popped off two quick shots and the machine gun was silenced, at least for now.

"Good job, kid," he said. "Keep your eyes open. Now, let's get moving. New Jersey, stick with us."

They kept advancing, Cole leading the way for Pomeroy and the kid, slowed now by the steep rise of the ground and the fire that was pouring down on them like a gale.

Off to his left, Cole glimpsed a couple of soldiers fall to their knees and then topple over. His mind went to that beach in Normandy, back in 1944, the way that blood and sand had mixed into a slurry at the water's edge. So many men had been lost on Omaha beach that to live had been the exception. The sight of those two boys going down had taken him back. Cole forced himself to snap out of it.

Everywhere along the American advance, the same scene of destruction was being repeated. This was terrible ground to attack and excellent ground to defend. The American attack seemed to be losing steam, but no one was calling for a retreat.

Even so, they were definitely getting stalled at the base of the ridge. Cole flung himself down again as bullets whistled overhead. The kid dove down next to him. Cole worked his elbows under him and put his sniper rifle to his shoulder. Their only hope was to pick off a few more of these machine gunners or otherwise thin the ranks of the defenders.

"Okay, search for targets," Cole said. "You call 'em as you seem 'em."

"Two o'clock," the kid said. "I think it's an officer." It was a target that was too good to pass up. Cole looked through the scope, saw a man who seemed to be giving orders to the others, and put his crosshairs on the Chinese soldier. The shot hit the officer square in the chest and he toppled forward down the slope.

"Got him," the kid said.

"Cole, what the hell are you doing here?"

Cole swiveled toward the voice, surprised to see Lieutenant Ballard nearby, crouched behind a rock.

"Couldn't let you have all the fun, sir."

"What are you doing with that rifle? What happened to Heywood?" Ballard demanded.

"Heywood's dead." Cole spat, clearing some grit from his mouth, or maybe the dead man's name had left a bad taste. "I picked up his rifle and thought I could do some good with it."

Ballard nodded. "Yeah, I saw how you picked off that officer. See if you can shoot a few more."

Sergeant Weber ran over and slid behind the rock like he was sliding into home plate. "We cannot stay here, sir," he said. In the excitement and stress of the moment, he sounded even more German than usual. "They will pin us down."

"You're right," Ballard agreed. He looked around as if trying to figure out where to direct his men in this crazy assault. Glancing behind him, Ballard's eyes quickly scanned the platoon and took stock of the men who had made it that far. His glance fell momentarily on Cole.

"See that machine gun up there, off to the left?" Ballard was referring to a heavy machine gun some distance away that had a field of fire that covered the ground the platoon needed to cross. In the sickly morning light, the green Chinese tracers stitched a deadly pattern across the killing field, reaching out to anything that moved. "He'll chew us to pieces if we try to move. Can you take him out? That's a hell of long way to shoot."

Cole got on the rifle. "Don't wait for me."

Ballard stood up and waved a hand to encourage his men forward into a hail of bullets. It was incredibly mad and incredibly brave.

Just as the deadly telltale tracers moved in Ballard's direction, Cole fired. The heavy machine gun fell silent and the platoon surged forward.

Cole stayed put and he reached out a hand to stop the kid before he could get up. On Cole's other side, Pomeroy hadn't made any effort to go anywhere.

"We'll do more good right here," he said. In Cole's accent, the last two words ran together and sounded like *rye cheer*. "We can pick off whoever we need to up on that ridge as soon as they poke their heads up and give us any trouble. Just your eyes open."

Cole quickly saw that the Chinese defenders had every advantage over the advancing platoon. Up on that ridge, they could throw down their stick grenades at the oncoming Americans, blasting yet more holes in the advance. He saw Ballard still leading the way, Sergeant Weber right behind him, leaping from rock to rock like a tough old billy goat. Cole reckoned those two must have charmed lives if they hadn't been hit yet.

Working against the Chinese was the fact that to fire down at this steep angle, they would need to expose themselves, which was to Cole's benefit. Whenever he saw an enemy soldier up on the ridge, he quickly dropped the man. Off to his right, the kid also called targets. Pomeroy popped off a few rounds at any soldiers who targeted Cole and the kid, who was armed only with binoculars.

To Cole's amazement, he saw that some of the enemy soldiers had gathered piles of large rocks, roughly the size of bowling balls, and were now lifting these rocks over their heads and hurling them down at the attackers. Their faces contorted with rage. Cole was reminded that this was how cavemen must have fought. Hurling the rocks was primitive but effective. One of those rocks was enough to bash in a head or break a man's shoulder when it struck from above.

Cole targeted one of the rock throwers and dropped him.

The attackers were not acting alone. Planes roared overhead, impossibly close. They could see the rivets on the underbelly of the planes. The planes strafed Sniper Ridge and the enemy positions hardly more than one hundred feet ahead of the American advance. Too close to use any bombs or napalm, but it was enough to decimate the Chinese defenders on the ridge.

There seemed to be fewer of them now. Were they melting away? He had heard that the Chinese had a network of tunnels and trenches, reaching deep into the ridge. Sneaky bastards that they were, maybe the Chinese had slipped away for now. They could regroup and stop the Americans at the next ridge, or the one after that. There was no shortage of hilltops to fight over.

He watched the lieutenant finally scramble up the last few feet, several men right behind him. They fired a few quick shots at whoever was left up there. Then the firing on the ridge came to a halt.

"I'll be damned," Cole muttered. "We done it."

* * *

WHILE HARDY FIDDLED with his camera, the American troops had prepared a final assault and surged up the last few feet of the ridge.

By then, many of the Chinese had simply melted back into the network of tunnels and trenches that the Americans were about to discover. After all, the enemy had occupied this position for weeks now, digging deeper into the ridge. They would simply use these tunnels to live to fight another day.

The few Chinese soldiers who remained behind put up a fight using their rifles and bayonets at close range, and finally some of them even started throwing rocks desperately at the attackers before they were shot down, one by one.

Hardy's ears rang, but the battlefield itself had suddenly fallen almost quiet in comparison to the previous din. Sniper Ridge now belonged to the American forces.

He looked back at the ground they had crossed reaching this place and saw the scattered bodies of both Chinese and Americans. His news-gathering mind prompted him to wonder how many. Too many to count. Dozens, anyhow. Several bodies lay across the concertina wire where they had created a bridge through that obstacle.

So many dead, he thought. The sight of the bodies shocked him, for he had never seen such a thing. He had read about this in books, but the reality of it took him completely out of himself. His emotions swirled. He felt sorrow, joy, pride. He fought the urge to weep, and then to laugh. Was this ridge worth the price? That wasn't something he could ponder in a news story. He realized the story that he would write needed to be about victory. He could puzzle out the exact words and approach later.

Meanwhile, Hardy took a deep breath and realized that he was just glad to be alive.

CHAPTER TWELVE

WITH THE CHINESE pushed off Sniper Ridge, the objective had been met and the advance against the enemy was halted. Some of the men stayed to hold the position, anticipating a counter-attack at any moment. The bulk of the men, Cole's battered squad among them, made their weary way back to the main encampment. Their role in the days ahead would be to plug holes as needed in the lines. Until then, they had a welcome chance for a hot meal and some sleep.

For Don Hardy, however, there would be no rest for the weary. He had been sent to this forward unit as a reporter, and now he had an article to write. He had to report on what had happened on the battlefield.

His first order of business was to secure a typewriter.

"You can use this one while I'm getting some chow," declared the same sergeant who had issued him the M-1 carbine. "The T and the H get hung up if you type too fast and the O is all gunked up, but you're welcome to have at it."

"Thank you, Sergeant."

"Hey, did you ever use that weapon?"

"Sure I did. I loaned it to one of the men who needed a crutch."

The sergeant shook his head, but he was grinning. "I just hope that you're a better writer than you are a soldier," he said. "That was one hell of a fight. Make us famous."

No sooner had the sergeant vacated his chair, then Hardy got to work. If his first order of business had been to secure a typewriter, his second order of business had been to find a large mug of coffee. Sure, Hemingway and more than a few other writers would have preferred a good slug of whiskey, but Hardy figured that would just put him to sleep.

Lucky for him, there was a large pot going in the headquarters tent and nobody seemed to mind if he helped himself. Somebody had left a cracked mug near the coffee pot. He filled the mug with coffee and guzzled it down, enjoying the hot liquid pouring down his parched throat, the rush of energy it gave him. He could have used something to eat, but that would have to wait for now. He poured another mug and got to work.

Like any young journalist worth his salt, he favored a good literary allusion. The snatch of poetry that had come to him on the battlefield returned for inspiration: *Into the valley of Death/Rode the six hundred ... Into the jaws of Death/Into the mouth of hell.* Where would he be without having had to memorize that Lord Tennyson poem back in high school?

Tennyson had been writing about the Crimean War a century ago, but aside from the lack of horses and sabres, Hardy supposed that war hadn't changed all that much.

He began to type. Quickly, he discovered that the sergeant had been correct about the keys sticking. In fact, they *all* got tangled up when he started to type too fast. As it turned out, not just the O was gummed up with old ink, but also the E and the P and the ... well, just about every letter. The ribbon was fading fast. Although Hardy knew how to type with his fingers spread across a QWERTY keyboard, the keys on the battered manual typewriter required so much effort to use that he was forced to use a two-finger approach so that he could hit the keys with enough force to make an impression on the page.

This slower act of writing enabled him to work in a few more poetic descriptions. He just hoped that the sergeant took his time in the mess tent so that he could finish typing.

Brave soldiers snatch victory from jaws of defeat at Triangle Hill

BY DONALD HARDY

Not since the six hundred rode into the Valley of Death in the famed poem by Lord Tennyson has such bravery been exhibited than at the battle of Triangle Hill on the morning of October 14, 1952.

On this day, soldiers of the storied 31st Regiment moved quickly to assault a strongly defended enemy position on a dusty hilltop called Sniper Ridge. Among those extremely battle-hardened troops were members of a rifle platoon commanded by Lieutenant Douglas C. Ballard

The enemy position at the top of the steep ridge was well-defended as our boys nobly attacked in the gray dawn, their guns flashing brightly and bayonets glinting wherever the pale dawn sun touched them like the fiery light of Olympus. The pop of gunfire was like Zeus himself cracking his knuckles.

"Keep it moving, keep it moving!" Lieutenant Ballard shouted commandingly, leading the way as his troops stormed the heights.

Among those soldiers was Tommy Wilson, who graduated from high school less than a year ago.

"Those Chinese are tough, but we're a whole lot tougher," he said as he fixed his bayonet to his rifle like a centurion of yore preparing to fight the barbarians with his shield and his spear.

As cannon behind them volleyed and thundered, each man of the squad had a story to tell, and perhaps a last letter home to write.

Another one of those soldiers was Caje Cole, a sniper of few words who prefers to let his rifle speak for him. More than a dozen of the enemy felt certain destruction dealt by his trusty rifle whenever his deadly sights fell upon them, firing as fast as his practiced hands could work the bolt action.

When asked how he could fire so quickly and accurately, he simply replied, "When I miss, I like to miss fast." Those words were delivered from one corner of his mouth, like an Old West gunfighter, before quickly turning back to the business of dealing out death to the enemy.

THE ARTICLE WENT on like that for a good eight hundred words of rather purple prose sprinkled liberally with half-remembered lines from the Tennyson poem and a crazy quilt of literary allusions. One of Hardy's English professors at Purdue had once complained that Hardy hadn't met an adverb or adjective he didn't like, and he didn't prove the professor wrong now. He would have kept on going with his poetic account now that the words and descriptions were flowing, but the sergeant had reappeared and needed his typewriter back to type up casualty reports.

In consolation, the sergeant had brought the reporter a sandwich.

"I figured you could use it," the sergeant said. "Typing on this thing is basically a wrestling match."

Hardy spooled out the sheets and stuffed them in an envelope, along with the roll of film that he had shot. There was no darkroom here on the front for developing film, even though Hardy had some skill with that.

He had used just one roll of the black-and-white film, because the editor had been explicit about not taking too many photos. It seemed that film cost money and took time to develop.

"If you shoot more than one roll of film, I'm going to shove that camera up your ass sideways," the editor had warned.

Then Hardy found a driver heading back to take this directly to the *Stars & Stripes* office. The guy wouldn't have done it, except that the sergeant was listening and helpfully offered to put his boot up the driver's ass sideways if he didn't cooperate.

Hardy reflected upon how it was a wonder that half the soldiers in Korea didn't walk around funny, with so many objects up their asses sideways.

Finally, Hardy wolfed down his sandwich, feeling that all was right in the world.

* * *

CHEN SAT SIPPING green tea by a low, smoking fire. The fire struggled to burn the knotty, stunted bracken that fed it, and the tea was mostly water, but a soldier did not complain about luxuries. He could thank Major Wu for the tea, and the fire, and even for a bowl of rice with salted fish. Wu, it seemed, was pleased with him.

Just two days ago, Chen had been with Wu up on that ridge, engaging with the imperialist snipers. He had killed one easily enough, in the way that he might crush a bug. Chen had simply snuffed him out.

But the second sniper had been different. This sniper had not only escaped with his life, which was an accomplishment in itself for anyone who fell under Chen's sights, but had come so close to shooting Chen that the experience had rattled him. It was not so much the fear of death in battle—Chen had long since come to accept that this might be his fate—as it was the fact that this American could shoot so well. Here, at least, was something more like an equal. Chen knew that this must be the sniper from the Chosin Reservoir. That thought did not cause him worry, but something closer to pleasant anticipation for the hunt ahead. He was sure that his dealings with the American were far from over. They had unfinished business, the two of them.

The wind shifted slightly, blowing the smoke into the faces of the other favored soldiers and staff, and making their eyes water. It was always windy in the mountains, gusts and eddies chasing themselves like wildcats at play, but Chen had been careful to sit on the western side of the fire, keeping the strongest winds at his back and assuring that the worst of the smoke would blow away from him.

After all, it was in Chen's nature to leave nothing to chance, at least what was in his control. In Chen's mind, even something such as where to sit at the fire must be weighed carefully. Every action that one took had a consequence. Also, there was the fact that any attack by the enemy would come out of the east. Facing in that direction, Chen's keen eyes would spot the enemy planes.

Neither did Major Wu's approach escape his detection. The political officer always managed to look like he was on dress parade. His green uniform with the flashes of red at the lapels reminded Chen of a peacock in a muddy barnyard, brilliant feathers against the drab. The uniform itself appeared spotless. Chen marveled at how the major managed to stay so clean here on the front lines. His own uniform was dirty, the original bleached cotton fabric long since gone a sooty gray, and well-worn, if not quite ragged.

"There you are," said Wu. The major always managed to be smiling, but it was like the smile of the mythical trickster, Sun Wukong, and not to be trusted. "I am glad that you are enjoying your tea."

"Yes, sir."

"Good, good. I am glad that you are rested because we have more work to do."

"Yes, sir."

"First, we will be taking some photographs this morning."

Chen had no idea what the major was talking about. Major Wu might have said that first they were flying to the moon this morning. Chen had never had his picture taken.

His face must have betrayed his confusion, because Wu laughed. "Yes, we are going to shoot you this morning, and it won't hurt a bit! Come, come!"

Chen gulped the last of his tea and hurried to follow Wu, who was already striding away. He grabbed his sniper rifle and followed. Quickly, another man who had been sitting on the smoky side of the fire moved to fill the space upwind that Chen had occupied. Chen reflected that this was a good lesson that in China, someone was always waiting to take your place.

Off in the near distance, in the direction of what the Americans called Sniper Ridge, Chen could hear firing and the occasional detonation of an artillery shell. Two days ago, the Americans had pushed the Chinese off that ridge. Despite his efforts as a sniper, and even though he had shot many of the enemy down like vermin, Chen and Wu had been forced to retreat with their comrades. However, the American victory had been short-lived. Just last night, Chinese forces had used the system of tunnels and trenches on that ridge to counter-attack. The ridge was now back in Chinese possession.

Wu began to climb in that direction, with Chen following. The major paused only long enough to wave over a soldier carrying a device that Chen supposed must be a camera. Chen was a peasant and a soldier—he had never seen such a thing up close and he felt nervous about having his photograph taken. How should he act?

They reached a spot below the ridge, out of sight of the enemy's prying eyes, but where there was still a background of hills and sky.

"This will do," Wu announced. "Do you see the landscape behind us? How majestic!"

"You could take someone else's photograph, sir," Chen suggested. His nervousness prompted him to speak; with an officer, especially a political commissar, it was best to do what one was told without question. Also, he felt some familiarity with Wu because they had shared many long hours together, hunting the enemy.

Wu merely smiled in that way of his, as if thinking of something amusing that he did not plan to share with you.

The major straightened up and looked around. They were close to one of the trails leading to the ridge, and it was busy with squads moving back and forth—fresh men headed toward the fight, broken and exhausted men heading back for at least a few hours of relief and a bowl of rice.

Wu pointed at one of the straggling soldiers limping back from the battlefield. "You there! Come here!"

Having been singled out, the man had no choice but to obey. Clearly puzzled about what the officer wanted, he limped toward Wu. It was evident from the bandage around his ankle that he had been wounded in some way.

Still, the man managed to pull himself into something that resembled coming to attention.

"Sir."

Wu glared at him, the habitual smile vanished. "Why have you abandoned your post?"

The soldier appeared mystified. "Sir? I was sent back?"

"You have sent yourself back," Wu stated. "This is a case of cowardice. You are a deserter."

"Sir, I am not a deserter," the soldier stammered, confused about what was going on. Like so many in the ranks, the soldier was no more than a simple peasant.

Wu drew his pistol and leveled it at the soldier's head. Nearby, Chen watched in disbelief. The soldier was clearly not a deserter. What was Wu playing at? What could he mean by this?

The spectacle taking place here drew some attention, and the passersby slowed to see what all the trouble was about. No one interfered, not even the officers. Wu's commissar's uniform was like a talisman.

"You know the penalty for desertion," Wu said, his pistol never wavering.

He pulled the trigger and shot the man.

Chen watched helplessly as the lifeless body sagged to the ground. One moment breathing, the next moment, dead at Wu's hand. He noticed that Wu stepped away from the gushing head wound to avoid getting blood on his boots. Chen thought that he heard the photographer beside him making whimpering noises.

The major turned to them. Chen surprised himself again by speaking up. "Was that man really a deserter, sir?"

"Of course not. But he was not useful to me—or to anyone else. Look around you. Does anyone care?"

A few of the troop on the trail glanced their way, but Wu was right —no one seemed to be too curious about the dead man at their feet.

"No, sir. No one cares."

"That man died because he was not useful to me, Chen. He was not useful to Chairman Mao. This is a good lesson for you that it is important to be useful. Now, let us take those photographs."

Under Wu's direction, Chen posed with his rifle, pretending to shoot at the enemy, while the photographer took his picture. Chen realized that Wu's demonstration had been a little too effective, judging by the nervousness of the photographer. The man could barely keep his hands from shaking in fear.

Major Wu had made his point, at the cost of a man's life. Be useful.

Today, all that Chen had to do was to pose with his rifle. Tomorrow, he would have to use that rifle and aim true. Do what he was told.

Otherwise, the message was clear that Wu might have a bullet waiting for him.

Once the photography session was over, Major Wu dismissed the photographer and turned to Chen.

"Now that we are finished here, you can get on with your real work, Chen. I won't be going with you today, however. I have other business to attend to." He paused, his trickster grin returning. "Remember what I said about being useful."

"Yes, sir."

"In other words, make these Americans pay for their imperialist arrogance."

Chen nodded, and began to climb the ridge to take up his position as a sniper.

* * *

TWO DAYS after Don Hardy had finished typing his opus on a borrowed typewriter, the result finally made it back to headquarters in the form of the newspaper. A few copies always found their way even to the front lines, and these were passed around. Lieutenant Ballard came through camp with a copy tucked under one arm. What stood out was the fact that Ballard was whistling.

"What's he so happy about?" Cole wondered.

"Oh, he's famous now," Pomeroy said, walking up from the other direction. "Or I ought to say that you're famous—there's a picture of you taking a shot with Ballard leaning over your shoulder."

"Yeah?"

"Yeah. That reporter fella was busy taking lots of pictures when we attacked that ridge."

What article didn't say was that the next day, the Chinese had taken back the ridge, pouring out of the network of defensive tunnels and trenches to overwhelm the attackers. Counter-attacks were surely being planned, but no one was eager for them.

Nobody was surprised. This was how the war in Korea worked, trading hilltops back and forth as the bodies piled up and the letters went home to the families of the dead.

With the two armies facing each other across the ridges, the enemy sniper had also gone back to work.

Orders came down for Cole. The enemy sniper had to be eliminated.

It was Lieutenant Ballard who brought him the news, along with a box of ammunition that he handed to Cole.

"Take him out," the lieutenant said.

CHAPTER THIRTEEN

COLE DIDN'T HAVE many fond childhood memories of growing up in Gashey's Creek, which had mostly been a hardscrabble existence, but the few good memories he had were mainly of going hunting in the morning. Those were always special mornings. He recalled being awakened before dawn by his father shaking his shoulder and saying gruffly, "C'mon, boy. You gonna sleep all day?" Never mind that it was still pitch dark out.

His father had not been a demonstrative man, but the closest that he'd come to affection was making sure that his boy wore two pairs of socks to keep his feet warm, and that he had a biscuit and a piece of venison jerky in his pocket. His father sometimes made him take along an apple or two, if they had any.

"I ain't that hungry."

"You'll want it later."

"What about you?" His pa rarely took anything to eat.

"A man ought to be a little hungry when he hunts. But it ain't right to make a young 'un go hungry."

He and his father headed out into the dawn, sometimes with one of his brothers, but usually just Cole and his father. As the oldest boy, it was a rite of passage to learn the woods and mountains in the same way that the Coles had been doing since the days of buckskin and flintlocks.

While it was true that his father was a failure at many things, including staying sober and providing for his family, he was a natural outdoorsman. He was what the old-timers called a woodsy. When he wasn't drinking the moonshine that he made back in the hills, his pa had been good at teaching Cole everything that he knew about the woods and the mountains and the animals that dwelt there. Cole had absorbed it all in the way that only young boys can, soaking up the lessons like the moss of the forest floor soaks up the rain.

Now on this autumn morning in Korea, he was going hunting again, but this time the game was far more dangerous. He was going after the Chinese sniper that had taken up residence on Sniper Ridge, which overlooked Triangle Hill and the American position.

The enemy sniper had picked off half a dozen men yesterday alone and was causing consternation among the Americans. While mortars and artillery did more damage, there was something intensely personal about a sniper. A lot of boys were just plain scared to poke their nose out of a trench or foxhole, and with good reason.

It was time to put an end to the sniper's reign of terror.

"Cole, I'm sending you up there to take care of that sniper once and for all," Lieutenant Ballard had said. "You know what? This isn't even coming from me. This comes directly from company HQ. They want that sniper over and done with. I told them, I have just the man for the job. Don't prove me wrong."

"Yes, sir," was all that Cole replied, hoping that the enemy sniper would cooperate and put himself in Cole's sights in short order.

He was taking Pomeroy with him this morning as a spotter.

"You ready yet?" he asked impatiently, looking toward where Pomeroy was stuffing a rucksack with a few things to bring along this morning. They had canteens, a handful of rations, and spare ammo, but aside from these essentials, they traveled light.

Cole had his rifle, of course, and Pomeroy carried binoculars to scan the opposite ridge. Cole's rangy legs warmed to the climb, while Pomeroy struggled a bit on his damaged feet—how he had managed to stay in the Army, Cole wasn't entirely sure. Either Pomeroy was a good liar, or else the military was so desperate for veteran soldiers that the doctors had agreed to return him to active duty when he asked. Pomeroy had gumption; he'd give him that.

They headed toward the front line. The camp around them was still sleepy and shaking off the dawn. The air felt chill, and they were glad for their jackets, but so far, the autumn days turned pleasantly warm once the sun had been up for a few hours.

No one challenged them on any of the paths up toward the ridge. Cole had found that carrying a scoped rifle eliminated most questions. Nobody felt inclined to ask a sniper for too many details.

"What did you have in mind this morning, Hillbilly?" Pomeroy asked.

"I reckoned we should start out in the sector that the sniper shot up yesterday," Cole said.

"You think he'll return to the scene of the crime?" Pomeroy asked, a little surprised. "I thought you said that snipers like to move around."

"I don't know if he'll be back," Cole admitted. "It wouldn't necessarily be a good idea to return to the same place, but he knows he's got himself easy pickings up there. Nobody was even shooting back at him."

"Might not be so easy this morning once we get there," Pomeroy said.

"That's the plan," Cole agreed. "But let's see how it turns out. He might pick an entirely different section to hunt in today."

"Hunt in? That's one hell of a way to put it. Hunting for our guys."

They climbed higher up the ridge, the exercise keeping them warm against the morning nip. They tried not to break a sweat, though, because sitting around in their damp clothes was a sure-fire way to feel chilled to the bone.

The morning was cool, but nothing like the Chosin Reservoir had been last winter. It had gotten so cold that the gun oil froze inside of rifles, rendering them useless. Some men who lacked proper winter gear had frozen to death in their foxholes. Their staring eyes frosted with a rime of ice wasn't a sight that Cole was going to forget anytime soon.

And that was just the cold. The situation had been compounded by nearly suicidal assaults by waves of Chinese troops, some of whom hadn't even been carrying weapons.

Cole glanced over at Pomeroy, who had been there alongside him at that godawful place. The kid had survived it, too. It was hard to get the memory or the chill of that place out of your bones. Cole shuddered all over again, just thinking about it.

"Hold up," Pomeroy said, breathing hard.

"You got to cut back on them coffin nails."

"Yeah, yeah."

They both paused for a few minutes and drank from their canteens, catching their breath. The sky had taken on a pale pink tone above the crest of the hills. A hunter's dawn, if ever there was one, Cole thought. He took that as a good sign.

When they reached the top of the ridge, they could see the line of soldiers dug in, facing the enemy position on the opposite hill. The soldiers looked about how you might expect, which was cold and miserable. Nobody gave him and Pomeroy a second look, except for a sergeant, who waved them over.

"Glad you're here," the sergeant said. He looked to be a tough old bird, with an unlit cigar clamped between square teeth. "Can you hit something with that rifle, or is this just another headquarters show?"

Cole ignored that and asked, "Where's he at?"

"He was right across from us yesterday," the sergeant replied. "Couldn't see him, but he sure as hell could see us. That son of a bitch killed some good men up here."

"I'll see what I can do," Cole said.

The sergeant looked him up and down, gazing for a moment at the Confederate flag painted on Cole's helmet, and then said, "Damn boy, I believe you just might know how to use that rifle, after all."

"We'll see."

They moved along the American position, seeking out a good place to set up. Cole was looking for cover and concealment. There was plenty of that to be found on this rocky, boulder-strewn ridge.

Finally, they reached a section of trench that nobody else seemed to want and they crawled into it. The bottom was muddy, and the hole smelled strongly of urine, but it was roomy enough for them both and positioned well for a clear view of the opposing ridge.

"Home sweet home," Pomeroy said. "All this place needs is maybe some new curtains and a throw rug."

He moved away from Cole and dug the binoculars out of the haversack.

However, Cole had a few arrangements to make first, none of which involved new curtains or throw rugs. Using the weak light of dawn as cover, when hopefully he would still be hidden from prying eyes, he crawled back out of the trench and arranged several rocks along the rim, doing it as artfully as he could so that it wasn't obvious that he had built himself a little wall there. He left just enough of a gap for him to put his rifle through.

Of course, the barrel of the rifle itself was wrapped in a strip of faded khaki cloth to help it blend into the surroundings. A few feet away, to Cole's right, Pomeroy would have enough of a gap to glass the enemy position with the binoculars, also wrapped in strips of cloth. Pomeroy could get the big picture and direct Cole to any activity over there.

Several hundred feet separated the ridges. They could certainly see any enemy soldiers over there without using binoculars or the scope, but it would have been hard if not impossible to hit anything using open sights. The sight itself would have blotted out the ant-like figures.

In the distance between the two ridges lay the shallow valley that the American soldiers had stormed across just days ago in their attack on Sniper Ridge. They had pushed the Chinese off for less than twenty-fours hours before a Chinese counter-attack put the ridge back in enemy hands.

Thinking about the men who had died that morning, it was a bitter pill to swallow, but that was Korea for you, Cole thought. Nothing more than a game of tug of war.

"What do you think?" Pomeroy asked. "Good spot?"

"I reckon it's as good as any," Cole said.

It was true that from where they were located, they could see much of any activity up and down Sniper Ridge. Of course, that activity on the part of the enemy would be limited once full daylight arrived, along with the American planes that would punish the enemy position as much as possible.

However, the planes had to be careful because some of the Chinese positions were now well defended and even included anti-aircraft guns, creating an unpleasant surprise at times for the pilots. There were even rumors that the Chinese were getting their own jets, some kind of Soviet fighter called a MiG, but they had yet to see one in the skies.

There was no doubt that the longer the war went on, the better equipped that the Chinese seemed to be, thanks to their Soviet allies. The Soviets were not providing the Chinese with first-rate weaponry, possibly in fear that the Chinese might in turn use it against the Soviets. However, the Chinese were welcome to their military castoffs and surplus from the last war.

Pomeroy already had the binoculars to his eyes. "Look at that," he said. "I already see something moving. Your two o'clock. Looks like three guys carrying stuff, maybe chow to their buddies in the trenches."

Cole eased the rifle that way and picked them up in the scope. He could, in fact, see two men making their way through the trenches over there, their heads and shoulders visible, but as they crossed an open area he saw that they were indeed carrying what might have been pails of food.

They would have been easy enough targets, but Cole took his finger off the trigger. He wasn't out here this morning to shoot the mess crew. He was here to target an enemy sniper and he wasn't ready to give away his own position just yet.

He knew that the element of surprise was worth a great deal. It wouldn't be easy and Cole hated to do it, but he planned to let the enemy marksman fire first at an unsuspecting American boy. He needed to draw out the enemy like poison from a wound.

Awful as that plan was, Cole knew that the sniper would then have revealed himself. Hopefully, Cole would then be able to put his crosshairs on the enemy sniper and eliminate him for good.

Cole bided his time, but his trigger finger was getting itchy.

CHAPTER FOURTEEN

DUTIFULLY, Pomeroy was working the enemy defenses with the binoculars.

"What I'd like to know is this," Pomeroy began. "Why did you drag me out here this morning? You should have brought the kid. He worships the ground you walk on, you know. He can't help it; he's easily impressed. Unlike me. If you had wanted him to, he would have shined your boots out here while you were at it."

Cole didn't say anything for a moment, not quite sure how he felt about someone supposedly worshiping the ground he walked on. He sure as hell didn't deserve that and it worried him a little. Deep down, he also suspected that Pomeroy was right about that.

"Listen here, New Jersey. I brought you along because you know what the hell you're doing and you don't get excited about it," Cole said. "Also, if the fat falls in the fire, I know that I can count on you."

"What fat and what fire?" Pomeroy wanted to know. "I wish you damn hillbillies would just speak plain English."

"The fat and fire I'm talking about is if the Chinese attack," Cole said. "They already took back Sniper Ridge. What if they want this ridge, too? You just never know when they'll turn the tables on us."

"Well, thanks for that," Pomeroy said. "I mean, who would want to miss maybe getting bayoneted, mortared, and shot when he could have been sleeping all nice and cozy in his tent this morning? You are a hell of a guy, Hillbilly."

"That's about what I thought you would say," Cole replied.

"What do you think? Is he out there this morning?" Pomeroy wanted to know.

Cole took his eye away from the scope long enough to scan the distant ridge. The light had grown quickly, picking out details that had been obscured in shadow just minutes before. The sense he had was like the woods on the morning of a hunt. Sometimes you could just feel a buck out there waiting for you in the shadows. At any moment, he would step into a clearing and present the perfect target. It got so you could tell right away whether or not a hunt was going to be successful.

Cole sniffed the air, enjoying the rich tang of fall. If there hadn't been a war on, it might have been a decent morning. At the same time, some part deep within him thought, *Who are you joshin'? You love every bit of this, right down to getting one of those enemy soldiers in your sights. If the other soldier is hunting you back, even better.*

Pomeroy was still awaiting his answer, so Cole said, "Oh, I reckon he's out there, all right. He's like us. He's been out here since first light, already in position and waiting."

"Did you seriously tell all that by sniffing the air?" Pomeroy wondered. "What are you, some kind of wolf? A coyote, maybe?"

Cole snorted. "Maybe I am something like that."

Pomeroy didn't reply, thinking that over.

As it turned out, he had plenty of time to ponder while they waited for something to happen. Cole went back to the scope and Pomeroy scanned the enemy ridge with the binoculars. The morning calm would likely lull some poor American boy into carelessness. He would show himself; there would be a rifle crack as the opposing sniper opened up business for the day. With any luck, Cole would shoot back.

As it turned out, they didn't have to wait long. The report of a rifle broke the morning quiet in the way that an egg is tapped against the side of a bowl, releasing the yolk. The rifle shot was followed by excited shouts and then a single cry for a medic.

When the call for a medic wasn't repeated, Cole figured that the poor boy shot by the Chinese sniper most likely wasn't going to be needing a medic, after all, because he was already gone.

The enemy sniper had taken the bait. The question was, could Cole now bring him down?

"If I didn't know better, I'd say he was almost directly across from us," Pomeroy said in a hoarse whisper, not taking his eye from the scope. "Anyhow, that's where it sounded like the shot come from. There was some echo in there, but if I was gonna bet, I'd say that's the spot, right around one o'clock."

"That's about what I thought, too," Cole said. "It's hard to see anything over there."

"Yeah," Pomeroy agreed. "You want rocks, I can find you lots of those. Enemy snipers, not so much."

"Keep looking," Cole said.

Not much after that, the enemy sniper fired again, picking off another soldier. Cole tried to ignore the cries of agony that, mercifully, did not last long.

"Definitely right across from us," Pomeroy said. "No doubt about it."

"Yep," Cole agreed.

However, pinpointing the sniper's hiding place would be more than a little difficult. As Pomeroy had pointed out earlier, the entire ridge was nothing more than a jumble of rocks and stunted brush with a few boulders thrown in for variety. He could be hiding anywhere in that mess. It went without saying that the enemy sniper would be as well-discussed as Cole, his rifle wrapped in cloth to break up its outline.

The only consolation was that looking across at the American lines, the sniper wouldn't be able to tell where he and Pomeroy were, either. There was simply too much territory to cover.

After a while, Pomeroy put down the binoculars and had a drink from his canteen. He dug around in the rucksack and found a half-eaten chocolate bar. He picked away some dirt and sawdust that was stuck to it and then started munching. "You want anything?"

"No," Cole said. The truth was that he liked to be a little hungry when he hunted. It kept his senses sharp. His pa had taught him that much on their morning hunts in the mountains. Those mornings seemed like a lifetime ago, but in reality it hadn't been much more than ten years. So much had happened since then.

Once Pomeroy had finished his snack, he suggested, "Should we try the old helmet on a stick?"

"That's about the dumbest idea I've heard in a while. He ain't gonna fall for that."

"All right, then," Pomeroy said. "Have it your way. We'll wait him out and let him pick off a few more of our boys."

Another hour went by before Cole said, "I guess you'd better find a stick."

Pomeroy found one. "My helmet or yours?"

"It was your idea, New Jersey, so we'll use your helmet."

"I was afraid you'd say that," Pomeroy said.

There was a reason that the helmet on a stick was one of the oldest tricks in the book. First of all, you didn't need any special equipment, just someone dumb enough to hold onto the helmet while it was raised into a sniper's line of sight. Second, from a distance it was hard to tell if the helmet was a ruse or not. A helmet was also hard to resist as a target. What rat didn't like cheese?

Cole kept his eye pressed tight to the scope, focused on the general area where he suspected that the other sniper was hiding. He waited, but nothing happened.

"Jiggle it up and down," he told Pomeroy.

Pomeroy did that, but nobody took the bait. Finally, Pomeroy lowered the helmet and put it back on his head, being careful to stay below the rim of the trench.

"Any other bright ideas?"

"I'll think about it," he said. "Now keep your eyes open."

It was just possible that they were too far away, and that the helmet was too small of a target for the enemy sniper to see.

Then again, maybe he just wasn't going to fall for it?

Cole didn't have other tricks up his sleeve at the moment. He settled down to wait. If nothing else, he was patient.

"What the hell are those guys doing?" Pomeroy asked.

"What guys?"

"Over there on the left."

Cole watched, incredulous, as a squad left the relative safety of the defenses and moved into the no-man's land between the two ridges. They were probing the enemy position, which wasn't all that unusual. It was what happened whenever some officer got bored. Cole had been on the short end of that particular stick more than a few times himself.

With an enemy sniper active, this was nothing but foolhardy.

The men picked their way down the slope. Their job was to approach the enemy defenses but not actually attack. They were to draw fire to help determine where the defenses on the ridge were strongest. Basically, they were decoys.

The Chinese dropped a mortar round or two from the top of the ridge, but the squad was out of effective mortar range. They were also too far away for anyone but a really good marksman to hit, so there were only a few desultory shots from the ridge. These were quickly silenced. Apparently, the Chinese were telling their men to hold their fire and not waste ammunition.

Cole realized that he was holding his breath. When the sniper didn't fire right away, he remembered to breathe again.

"Maybe he packed it in already," Pomeroy said.

But that turned out to be wishful thinking. No sooner had the squad entered the tangle of barbed wire below and started picking their way through, then a rifle shot rang out. One of the soldiers below threw back his arms and collapsed.

The others ran for cover, but there wasn't much down there to hide behind other than more barbed wire. Some threw themselves flat or got into shell holes, but not before the sniper had fired again, dropping another man.

Two shots. Two men down. This son of a bitch didn't miss.

"This is goddamn awful. They're sitting ducks down there," Pomeroy said. He glassed the opposite ridge desperately. "I think I see him. Got a little puff of smoke or something. Just past that old tree."

Through the scope, Cole spotted the gnarled tree. Stripped of any vegetation, the bark had been shredded by bullets and shrapnel. And then he saw just a hint of motion. It wasn't the sniper, he realized. It was someone with a pair of binoculars. Like Cole, the enemy sniper must also have a spotter. He didn't see a helmet, which was interesting; the spotter seemed to be wearing an officer's hat with a splash of red on it. What kind of sniper was important enough to have an officer calling the shots for him?

The kind of sniper that didn't miss, that's who.

Straining through the scope, he tried to pick out something that might be the sniper. However, the man was too hidden. Although he could see the spotter, that's not who he wanted to shoot. The sniper would just find another one.

He noticed the spotter's head tilt to the right, as if talking to someone one. Cole still couldn't see the enemy sniper, but he picked a spot four feet to the right of the spotter, and fired. He worked the bolt and fired again for good measure.

Even if he couldn't possibly hope to hit the enemy sniper, Cole could give him something to think about by sending a couple of bullets in his general direction.

But in the process, he had managed to give himself away. Maybe there had been a glint off the lens of his telescopic sight. Maybe it was a glint off Pomeroy's binoculars.

Whatever the case, a bullet came in and he heard Pomeroy go, "Unnhh." Delayed, he heard the crack of the distant rifle shot an instant later.

He still hadn't seen a thing, so he put down the rifle and turned toward Pomeroy. He was sitting in the mud at the bottom of the trench, clearly stunned, one hand pressed to the side of his head. Blood ran between his fingers.

"You're hit, you're hit!" Cole said, crawling toward him. He pulled Pomeroy's hand away, afraid of what he might see.

Pomeroy's hand looked managed, and also his ear. A ribbon of torn flesh dangled from it. Some of his scalp was ripped up. Miraculously, the bullet had just missed his skull.

Cole realized what had happened. Pomeroy had probably let down his guard and stood too far above the trench to get a better view. He had still been holding the binoculars when the bullet had hit his left hand and then his ear.

"How bad is it?" Pomeroy asked.

"You'll be all right," Cole said. "Missed your head. Chewed up your ear and some of your fingers."

In Cole's mountain drawl, it came out as *fangers*.

"Hurts like hell."

Pomeroy's ear and scalp were also bleeding like hell, with blood running down his neck and soaking into his uniform tunic. Cole shouted, "Medic!"

He got a gauze pack and used it to staunch some of the flowing blood. A medic was running toward their position, stooped over as far as he could go, hoping to dodge the next bullet.

To give the medic a better chance of reaching them in one piece, Cole got back on the rifle and put a round into the spot where he thought the sniper might be hiding. This time, the spotter was nowhere to be seen.

"Dammit that stings," Pomeroy said. "The worst part is that they'll send me home now for sure."

"Some folks have all the luck," Cole said.

CHAPTER FIFTEEN

WOUNDED AND BLEEDING, Pomeroy was too dizzy to walk himself down the ridge to the field hospital. The medic wrapped his hand and bandaged his head, then called for a stretcher.

"We'll have to carry you down part of the way," the medic said. "It's too steep for an ambulance to get up here."

"I can walk," Pomeroy said, but he didn't sound all that convincing. His eyes had gone a little glassy.

"Good thing you've got a hard head," Cole said. He never had been good at jokes or small talk, but this was one time where he felt like he had to try. What he didn't say was that if the bullet had gone an inch in the other direction, Pomeroy would've been a goner. He didn't have to say it because they both knew it.

A couple of stretcher-bearers came along. They were black soldiers because the military claimed to be integrated but gave jobs like this to them, rather than combat roles. They managed to get Pomeroy loaded on the stretcher. Everybody kept their heads down because the sniper was still out there, for all they knew.

Just as they started down the slope, Pomeroy told them to wait. He waved Cole over.

"You have got to get that sniper," he said, suddenly clutching at Cole's arm. "Don't let him shoot anybody else."

"I reckon I'll try," Cole said.

"It's up to you, Hillbilly. Nobody else can do it. It ends here and now."

Finally, Cole promised to find him later at the field hospital, and the stretcher-bearers carried Pomeroy away.

Cole crept back into the trench. He rarely felt at a loss, or uncertain about what to do next, but he did now. He needed to regroup. For a long time, he just sat in the bottom of the hole, his back to the wall and his rifle propped between his knees. He felt that he had let Pomeroy down in some way. Sure, Pomeroy was lucky to be alive, but he'd be a whole lot luckier if he hadn't gotten shot in the first place.

When he was ready to get back on the scope, he slipped out of the trench and into a new position, crawling in among some boulders. There was no point in making it any easier for the enemy sniper than necessary by staying in a position where he knew Cole to be. He stretched out on his belly, keeping low to the ground.

Cole positioned the rifle so that the muzzle barely protruded beyond the rocks. It would have taken eagle eyes to spot him. Meanwhile, he put his crosshairs over the spot where he had spotted the enemy sniper earlier. However, there was no sign of movement. If the sniper had any sense, then had found a different location from which to shoot, just as Cole had done.

If he was even there at all. As the day's shadows lengthened, no more bullets came from the opposite ridge. Perhaps the enemy sniper had called it a day. Clouds built to the west and began to move up and cover the sun, dispelling any of the autumn day's warmth. As the ridge slipped into shade, the wind picked up and Cole felt the cold begin to seep up through the ground. A rock was digging into his ribcage, but he ignored it. He felt a few hunger pangs and ignored those as well. The only concession to comfort was taking a few sips from his canteen when his mouth started to feel dry as cotton. The metallic-tasting water was not exactly refreshing.

What most people didn't know or understand about being a sniper, especially someone like Lieutenant Ballard, was that being able to shoot and hit a target was only part of it. Being a sniper required patience. Being a sniper also required a certain ability to turn off all those signals of discomfort that the body normally sent. That you were cold, or hungry, or that your bladder was full. All that mattered was the circular world that he saw through the rifle scope.

Cole tightened his grip on the rifle, feeling the familiar texture of the wood grain with its dings and divots from hard use. Staring through the scope for so long, without so much as blinking, was exhausting. He was glad when it started to get dark, putting an end to the day's business. *Can't shoot what I can't see.* He backed out of his hidey-hole like a spider.

* * *

THE RED EVENING sky touching the mountaintops had faded to black and purple as Cole got back to the camp, then made his way down to the field hospital to check on Pomeroy. He found him there on a row of cots, looking miserable, and heavily bandaged.

"Did you nail him?" was the first thing that Pomeroy wanted to know.

"No," Cole said. "He didn't show himself again."

"I meant what I said. You've got to settle his hash."

"I will," Cole said, although the words sounded doubtful to his own ears. Something about that Chinese sniper had rattled him. He decided to change the subject.

Leaning in to take a closer look at Pomeroy's heavily bandaged face, he concluded, "I've got to say, that's a face that could drive rats from a barn."

Pomeroy groaned. "Spare me the hillbillyisms."

"Ain't nothin' hillbilly about that. It's the simple truth."

"Yeah, well, I won't be here long for you to make fun of. Doc says they're gonna fly me out to Seoul, or maybe even to Tokyo."

"You done that before," Cole said, thinking of Pomeroy's serious case of frostbite after the Chosin Reservoir. During that campaign, Pomeroy had also been hit by shrapnel, receiving a flesh wound in the side. He was starting to think that maybe Pomeroy had nine lives. "Them doctors fixed you right up last time, and they will again."

"I won't be coming back this time, Cole. They wanted to send me home after the frostbite, but I talked my way out of it. I thought that I could still do some good. This time, I'm going home."

"I reckon you deserve it."

"I'd tell you to look me up sometime when you get back to the states, but I think that you'd just scare my wife and kid."

"Don't worry about me, New Jersey. You go on home and make sure they treat you right."

"There's not a whole lot waiting for me at home," Pomeroy admitted. "Why the hell do you think I came over here."

"It's time for a fresh start, then. Ain't never too late for that."

Pomeroy nodded, thinking it over. "Maybe you're right."

"Damn straight I'm right. Get some rest, New Jersey. I'm heading back out first thing in the mornin' after that Chinese sniper, but I'll see you tomorrow night."

Cole headed out of the hospital, but not before stopping to ask an orderly if they had brought in anyone else from Sniper Ridge.

He pointed at a cot. "That poor bastard there was the only one. There's some Chinese sniper up there who doesn't miss much."

"So I've heard."

Cole went and stood by the wounded soldier's cot. He was heavily bandaged; it looked to Cole as if he'd been hit in the neck. The soldier had his eyes closed and appeared to be sleeping soundly.

"Is he gonna make it?" Cole asked quietly.

"Maybe, although he might wish he hadn't. Doc says he won't talk again, shot in the neck like that."

Cole shook his head and got out of there, thinking that the Chinese sniper had to go. In the morning, he would try again.

* * *

CHEN RETURNED to camp that evening with a sense of satisfaction. He had performed his duties as a sniper by slaughtering more of the imperialist soldiers. This pleased him, just as it seemed to please Major Wu.

As a result, Chen found himself back at a campfire, allowed to warm his bones at the fire while most soldiers shivered in the growing dark. Although it was only October, the nights in the mountains had grown increasingly chill. Chen suspected that when they awoke in the morning, that they would find a frost—the air had that edge of dampness to it and there was little wind.

He was given a bowl of rice into which a bit of meat had been mixed. Chen chewed the gristly meat, trying to determine its origin, and decided that it was better not to think too much about it. He had seen some horses around the camp yesterday, but come to think of it, he had not seen them this evening. He ate the bowl to the last grain of rice without complaining.

Someone pressed a bottle into his hands, and Chen took a couple of swigs of liquor. He never had cared too much for alcohol, but he was grateful for the warmth it provided this evening. He felt the fiery glow spread through him and very nearly felt content.

One thought that nagged at him concerned the American sniper that he had encountered today. The thought of that other sniper was like a shadow lurking beyond the firelight. The man had seemed to know just where Chen would be. The shots that he had fired at Chen had come close.

Then again, Chen was more than a helpless target. He had managed to shoot back.

Chen was sure that he had not managed to shoot the enemy sniper, but he had definitely hit the spotter. Had he been lucky enough to kill the spotter? It was hard to say.

"You got him!" Major Wu had said gleefully, peering through his binoculars at the American position.

"What about the sniper?"

"Maybe that was him? I will certainly say so, in my report."

"I don't think that was the sniper, sir."

Wu just smiled. "Of course it was! And if it wasn't, I will report that the sniper you kill tomorrow is a different one."

"Yes, sir."

In fact, Wu had been so confident that they had ended their work early for the day, which was why Chen was now sitting here by the fire.

But Chen knew that Wu could write all the reports that he wanted, but that the American sniper would still be out there. Chen would have another chance at him tomorrow.

The bottle came round again, but Chen simply passed it along. He did not need a wooden head in the morning, not with the enemy that he faced.

Instead of sitting by the fire and drinking, he moved some distance away and spread out his blanket roll. His front still felt some warmth from the fire, but his back felt cold. Next, Chen began cleaning his rifle.

There wasn't much else to occupy his time. He had to admit that back before he had become a communist, army life was more fun. Gambling had been allowed back then, for example. The stakes were never high, but it was a way for soldiers to pass the time. Drinking was allowed to some extent only because there was only so much austerity that the soldiers could stand. Women could be bought cheaply.

At that time, no one wrote letters home. Most of the Chinese soldiers could neither read nor write, anyhow, and that included Chen. Besides, there was nothing like a postal service. The only way that a letter made it home was by giving it to someone who might be returning to your home province. Eventually, being passed from one person to the next, the letter would find its way to the right person. The communist government had no postal service because it preferred its citizens not being able to communicate—communication only meant trouble.

Chen was still cleaning his rifle when Major Wu appeared. Wu was rarely alone, and this time was no exception. With him was one of the military advisors from the Soviet Union. There were several such men in camp. Their role was to observe the Chinese in battle and provide training for some of the Chinese troops using the antiquated military gear provided by the Soviet Union. Mostly, the Soviet observers simply watched, serving as Stalin's eyes and ears.

"There you are!" Wu said, grinning. Chen suspected that the grin was similar to that of a fox that had just entered a farmyard filled with chickens. "Have you eaten?"

This was the universal question that all Chinese asked one another, even if one man was a political officer, and the other was a simple marksman with a rifle.

"Yes, sir," Chen replied. "I am grateful."

Wu nodded, beaming as if he had prepared the bowl of horse meat and rice himself.

"This is one of our brothers from the Soviet Union," Wu explained, gesturing at the Red Army soldier. The man's face remained impassive, so it was difficult to tell whether or not he understood a word of Chinese. "I wanted to show him what one of our snipers looks like."

Wu turned to the Soviet officer, and with a few halting words in what must have been Russian, and with gestures, he conveyed his information to the man.

Chen had detached the scope from his rifle, and the Soviet officer picked it up and looked it over carefully. Smiling, the man said something in Russian back to Major Wu, then laughed.

Wu laughed back, as if what the Soviet officer had said to him was amusing. Then Wu communicated something more to the Soviet, who only raised his eyebrows in the universal expression of surprise.

The Russian handed back Chen's rifle scope, this time with an unmistakable air of deference—the man was obviously impressed by whatever Wu had told him.

Major Wu explained to Chen, "He said he wonders how many imperialists were last seen alive through this sight. I told him that you shot ten enemy soldiers today!"

Chen was taken aback. "Sir, it could not have been more than four or five. Some may only have been wounded."

Still smiling, Wu responded, "Chen, how many times must I tell you? However many kills I put in my report, that is how many that you have shot."

"Ten men, sir."

"That is correct," Wu said. "Carry on cleaning your rifle, Chen. Then get some rest. Tomorrow morning, we will go hunting again. You can shoot that American sniper all over again, if need be."

CHAPTER SIXTEEN

COLE STEPPED FORTH into the cold gray light of dawn. There was none of the anticipation that he had felt yesterday. None of the excitement of the hunt. Certainly, he did not pause to revel in any memories of heading out at first light to hunt with his father. No, this morning felt like he was slogging his way toward a duel or maybe to an execution—hopefully not his own.

"Stick with me and keep your head down, kid," he murmured to Tommy Wilson. He wanted to keep the kid within whispering distance because sound traveled far on the morning air. A few wisps of cold mist drifted close to the ground. The air dragged at them, feeling heavy and cold.

"How far have we got to go?"

Cole paused long enough to nod at the peak ahead. "There's a place where I want to set up on yonder ridge."

"Isn't that near where you set up yesterday?"

"Thereabouts."

"Won't he be expecting you, then? The other sniper, I mean."

"That's the whole idea, kid. We've got to find each other to try and kill each other."

The kid didn't have an answer to that, so they kept heading up the trail. The slope was gradual at first, but would rise more steeply the closer that they came to the ridge.

Cole had mixed emotions about dragging the kid into this mess. On the one hand, the kid was dependable and would do what Cole told him. He had enough sense to keep his head down or he wouldn't have survived this long. A lot of soldiers hadn't—the life expectancy wasn't exactly long for a greenbean fresh from boot camp. But even Cole had to grudgingly admit that the kid was no greenbean anymore. Tommy Wilson had trudged his way out of the Chosin Reservoir with the best of them. Since then, he had seen plenty of action as part of the rifle squad.

On the other hand, Cole was wary of this Chinese sniper that he was about to confront. That son of a bitch could shoot like nobody's business and he was slippery as an eel. More than likely, it had been this same sniper who settled Heywood's hash. Yesterday, the sniper had damn near killed Pomeroy. Another inch and, well, that would have been that.

Cole hadn't been able to protect Pomeroy, who was a seasoned veteran. How the hell was Cole supposed to protect the kid?

As far as Cole was concerned, all bets were off.

"Like I said, kid, keep your head down and don't take any chances today," he found himself saying. He didn't add that he had almost gotten Pomeroy killed yesterday, so didn't want to see the kid added to the casualty list.

The ground rose and their leg muscles began to get a workout. Cole's breathing deepened, sounding loud as a forge bellows in the quiet morning, although that was likely just his imagination. Good thing they were traveling light. Cole had his rifle and spare ammo, a canteen filled with lukewarm metallic-flavored water, and some rations stuffed in his pockets. The kid carried about the same, along with the binoculars. Miraculously, they were unscathed after yesterday's close call, which was a good thing because a decent pair of binoculars was hard to come by on the front lines. The binoculars seemed to be fine, except for Pomeroy's blood dried into the nooks and crannies.

He approached the same trench where he had set up yesterday. Silently, he jumped down into it. The kid followed, but looked around a little mystified. The low wall was still set up, along with a rest that Cole had created, complete with an old folded sheet of canvas.

"Here?" Tommy asked. "It looks like some other sniper was already using this spot. Wait a minute—"

"Yeah, this is where I was yesterday. Now he'll know where to find me," Cole said.

Breaking every rule in his book, Cole was returning to the same location. Generally, a sniper who moved around survived because he wasn't expected in the same place. Routine led to danger—an enemy who knew your approach and exit routes might simply be waiting to pick you off. But Cole didn't expect that to be the case here. He'd had the sense this morning that he was headed to a duel, and he wasn't far off.

Cole did make a few adjustments, adding a few more stones in front of the trench where the kid was positioned. He was shorter than Pomeroy, anyhow, so that was something. As long as the kid didn't go sticking his head up, he ought to be fine.

Ought to be, Cole reminded himself.

It took Cole just a few minutes to set up and get his bearings. Through the scope, he studied the ridge in front of them. It looked about the same. He told the kid where the enemy sniper had been set up yesterday.

"That ain't to say he won't move around," Cole said. "Keep your eyes open."

"Maybe he won't even be there."

"Oh, he'll be there."

"How do you know?"

"He'll be there." To himself, he added *because he's just like me*.

Slowly, the defenses around them woke up for the day, now that it was getting light enough to see the enemy position. Any night when there hadn't been a Chinese surprise attack was a good one. Any morning when you woke up at all was a good one when you were on the front line.

Across from them, Sniper Ridge was coming into sharper focus. Beyond it stood the twin peaks of the hill known as Jane Russell, with Pike's Peak nearby. Cole thought that maybe Pike's Peak was back in

Chinese control—or had that been two days ago? It was hard to say because the two sides swapped faster than partners at a barn dance. *Dosey-doe, away we go.*

For now, the enemy was dug securely into the hilltop.

"I feel sorry for the poor bastards who have to push them off," he said. "All they had to do two days ago was throw rocks down at us."

"One step forward, two steps back," the kid agreed.

From time to time, a few bursts of artillery rained down on the ridge to help keep the Chinese pinned in place. The shells passed overhead with a sound like ripping paper before striking with an earth-shattering detonation. Not to be outdone, the Chinese released a few volleys of their own artillery fire back at the American positions.

Now that it was getting light, they could already hear the drone of approaching aircraft. A couple of planes came in low over the ridge off to the east, saying good morning to the enemy with a round of napalm.

It was lucky for the US and UN forces that they never had to worry about air superiority. There had been some noises about the Chinese having some planes, but they had never seen any.

"Give 'em hell, boys," Cole muttered, watching the hillside blossom with a bright orange fireball that billowed out into a gaseous ball before fading to shades of red and black. Shreds of burning flame were left behind on the mountainside as the fire claimed shrubs, scrub trees, and whatever else lay in its path—such as the Chinese soldiers occupying the trenches there.

From a distance, the bombing made for a captivating show. Up close, the bombing must have been terrifying. The slight breeze shifted, and after a while, Cole caught a whiff of the smell of the burning jellied gasoline. The stink of it roiled his stomach.

Their bombs dropped, the planes turned to circle over the American-held ridge. They waggled their wings, coming in low enough to make out the figure in the cockpit, then swept away toward the distant coast.

"I wouldn't mind being a pilot," the kid said. "That's got to be the easiest job in the world. Fly in, drop your bombs, fly back in time for dinner."

"Not so easy when you have engine troubles or when somebody decides to shoot at you."

"I'd take my chances," the kid said. "It's got to be better than being in a foxhole."

Cole was glad to keep his feet on the ground and on dry land, for that matter.

He turned his gaze back to the enemy's ridge, looking for targets.

They had come out here to get the attention of the enemy sniper. It was time to poke the hornet's nest. Short of being able to determine where the sniper was hiding—if he was even out there at all this morning—the next best thing was to pick off a few of the enemy soldiers. If he started doing that, then somebody would notice him, eventually.

Cole's practiced eye soon saw some movement on the ridge opposite them. Just as on the American side, the enemy troops were waking up and starting their day. That meant there were orders to relay. Messages to carry. Even rations to deliver, because the Chinese relied more on freshly cooked food than the US and UN forces, who had their packaged rations. From the evidence that they had found in abandoned or captured enemy defenses, it appeared that the enemy lived mostly on rice. Cole almost felt sorry for them. Rice was a hell of a thing to have to fight a war on.

The soldier he spotted was moving from foxhole to trench to boulder, keeping his head down as if he might have felt Cole's crosshairs tracking him. His grayish uniform and furtive movements made him resemble nothing more than an overgrown gopher.

At this distance, Cole did not want to attempt a moving shot. He kept his crosshairs on the man, following along with him as he disappeared behind cover and then reappeared, until the enemy soldier finally came to a halt. It was hard to say why he had stopped, and it really didn't matter.

Cole felt the rifle kick against his shoulder. The bullet required nearly one full second to traverse the distance between ridges, during which time the soldier did not move. Consequently, the bullet hit him and flung him around, as if he had been punched in the shoulder. He went down and did not get back up.

A little to the left next time, Cole thought.

"You got him!" the kid exclaimed, watching through the binoculars. He had pushed his glasses up out of the way and had his eyes right against the binoculars. Lowering the binoculars, he pushed the glasses back down and blinked as his vision adjusted. "Wow, that is really far. You know what, I can barely even see that far, especially without my glasses."

"Then you'd better not lose your glasses."

"Where did you learn to shoot like that?" the kid asked.

"Just comes natural, I suppose."

"You know, some people are just good at baseball. Or at football. But they also get plenty of practice."

Cole thought about it. "I practically grew up with a rifle in my hands," he admitted. "I can't even tell you how old I was when I first went into the woods by myself with a rifle."

"My parents would even let me have a BB gun," the kid said. "They were afraid I would shoot songbirds. Mom said it was bad luck to kill a sparrow. She was worried about me killing birds and look at me now, here in Korea."

"It's a hell of a thing, kid," Cole snorted. "Your folks might have let you take to the woods with a rifle if'n they'd been hungry enough and needed you to bring supper home."

"Not unless you could shoot a meatloaf."

Growing up in the mountains had been different, he supposed. There were always chores to do, from hauling water to feeding the hogs to taking a hoe to the garden. Had he ever really been a child? Not in the usual sense of being a carefree little boy. In the mountains, a child was something that you put to work earning his keep as soon as possible. A child was another mouth to feed.

As for taking to the woods with a rifle when he was barely big enough to carry it, his careworn mother didn't have much say in the matter and it was just possible that his old man had been too drunk to care, or off in the hills making moonshine.

Cole turned back to using the scope to scan for his next targets. Nearby, he knew that the kid was doing the same thing with the binoculars.

Something wriggled at the back of Cole's mind, thinking about the shot that he had just taken. The downed man was just another anonymous soldier, and yet he was like *every* soldier in some way. Cole had just taken away everything that the man ever had or ever would have. He had just deprived him of life.

It was a hard thing to think too much about. But killing is what he did. It's what any soldier did.

Whenever Cole felt himself growing soft, or reluctant to pull the trigger, he only had to remember the soldiers that he and Sergeant Weber had found frozen in their foxholes on the shores of the Chosin Reservoir, eyes iced over, or the screams of the wounded when the Chinese set fire to the trucks and ambulances they captured on the retreat from Chosin. Those memories hardened his heart.

To be sure, the Chinese had been particularly cruel. He supposed part of it was simple revenge. The attacking Chinese forces had been mown down in huge numbers. Although the enemy forces greatly outnumbered the Americans and their UN allies, the advantage in firepower clearly lay on the American side. A single BAR could cut a vast hole in the attacking line.

In fact, not all of the Chinese attackers back then had even carried rifles. The first wave had been armed, of course, mostly with inferior Chinese-made bolt-action rifles that were no match for the semi-automatic M-1 rifles and carbines used by the US troops.

The second wave of Chinese attackers were expected to pick up weapons from their fallen comrades. Their only weapons were stick grenades, strapped into special holsters or simply shoved into their pockets. Cole supposed that was better than nothing, but you had to get close enough to toss a grenade, and many didn't.

There was no going back, however. No retreat for the Chinese troops. The Chinese attacks had included a third wave made up of the political officers. This last group was well-armed with pistols and even submachine guns, but their role was not as assault troops. Instead, their mission was to shoot any soldiers from the first two waves who dared to retreat.

With those Chinese troops caught between a rock and a hard place, it was almost possible to feel sorry for them.

Once the enemy started overtaking the slow-moving US trucks on the single road leading from Chosin, they had turned the tables by slaughtering the wounded inside.

The Germans had been tough customers in the last war, and there had been brutal incidents like the Malmedy massacre at the Battle of the Bulge, but such war crimes were the exception. Even they drew the line at outright murder of POWs and wounded.

Soldiers captured alive by the Chinese or their North Korean allies had a good chance of staying that way because the Chinese wanted to keep them that way as negotiating pawns.

But the Chinese didn't want to be bothered taking care of any wounded. In fairness, they could barely take care of their own. But it was the way that they went about it that was so godawful. First, they fired through the canvas sides, and then they tossed in grenades or ran forward with torches to set the trucks ablaze.

Sons of bitches.

When he thought about those things, the screams of men being burned alive and the terrible smell of it, Cole didn't mind killing so much.

"Off to your right, about a hundred feet from the last one," said the kid, binoculars pressed to his eyes.

Cole glanced away from the scope just long enough to see that the kid was barely showing anything but the top of his helmet above the rim of the trench. He ought to be safe enough; the enemy sniper would need to be eagle-eyed to catch a glimpse of him.

Following the kid's directions, Cole looked through the scope and spotted that man as well. He put the crosshairs on him. He fired again, and again, reaping the enemy as soon as a target presented itself.

The kid was proving himself to be almost as much of a good spotter as Pomeroy had been, which was saying something. Of course, located as they were in the American lines, Cole and the kid could devote their full attention to the targets on the ridge. Nobody was going to be sneaking up behind him, which would have been a concern anywhere else.

"I've got to take a leak," the kid announced.

"Do it right here in the trench," Cole said.

"You sure?"

"Have you gotten a whiff of this hole, kid? You wouldn't be the first to use it as a latrine. Anyhow, you crawl out of this trench, and somebody is sure as hell gonna see you. That other sniper is out there. He knows I'm in the vicinity. No point in giving him something to shoot out."

A few moments later, he heard the kid's stream splashing down to mix into the mud at the bottom of the ditch. The kid kicked some dirt over it and got back on the binoculars.

Although there were a few desultory potshots from the Chinese line, nobody made any real effort to challenge Cole.

With the kid working as his spotter, he continued to pick off any enemy soldier who showed himself on the opposite ridge. He was like a turkey buzzard, picking clean the bones on a carcass—the carcass in this case being the enemy defenses.

There was no sign yet of the enemy sniper.

Where are you, you son of a bitch?

CHAPTER SEVENTEEN

COLE'S GLANCE slid to the kid, who was still glassing the ridge. "How long do we wait?" the kid asked. "Are we gonna stay here all day when there's nothing going on?"

"Maybe you want to head back to camp and take a nap while this sniper picks off whoever he wants," Cole snapped, sharper than he had intended, but the kid had gotten into his craw.

"Seems like a waste of time, is all," the kid muttered. "What sniper?"

Cole couldn't blame the kid. Not everyone possessed a sniper's patience. They had been at this now for a couple of hours, long enough for most of the cloud cover to burn off, except for a stubborn gauze. They could feel the warmth of the sun on their backs as they hunkered down in the hole. The warmth didn't help the smell. In Cole's experience, there wasn't much that smelled good in Korea. This hole surely wasn't one of the good places, with its stink of sour urine and cold mud.

He ignored the smell, staying focused instead on the circle of magnified landscape visible through his rifle scope. The scope moved over the ridge opposite them, the mid-morning light giving the enemy no shadows to lurk in. He had already picked off a few enemy soldiers. They were wise to him now, though, and nothing was moving.

Maybe the kid was right. Maybe the enemy sniper wasn't showing up today.

Somewhere behind him, he heard voices. This wasn't anything unusual because they were surrounded by other soldiers up here on the line, keeping an eye on the enemy. However, there was something familiar about one of the voices.

"He's up there, sir."

"All right. I'll find him."

Aw, hell. It registered now who that voice belonged to. A minute later, he heard that voice right behind him.

"Cole, we're coming to you."

He glanced behind him to see Lieutenant Ballard on his belly, using his elbows to drag himself across the open ground. Another man came behind him, and Cole recognized the reporter from the *Stars & Stripes*. He was also crawling, but with a camera in one hand, trying to keep it out of the dirt. Cole hadn't wanted the kid to leave the foxhole for fear that he would be a target, but if these two fools wanted to get shot, to hell with them.

The two men slithered forward into the hole. It had been crowded enough with just him and the kid. Now, they were packed together like sardines in a tin. Somebody accidentally jammed a knee into his back, throwing off his aim. He took his eye off the scope and glared balefully at Lieutenant Ballard.

The lieutenant didn't seem to notice, or maybe he didn't care. "Did you get that sniper yet?"

"Not yet, sir," Cole replied through gritted teeth.

"Well, keep trying. They're anxious about enemy snipers back at HQ. This one in particular. He shot six men yesterday. It's bad for moral. If you can't bag him, then you can go back to the mess tent and I'll find someone who will."

"Cole got a couple for us today to even the score," the kid said. "He just hasn't gotten that sniper yet, sir."

Ballard nodded. "Keep up the pressure, Cole. It's important.

Anyhow, I brought Hardy along to write about a sniper in action and how I came up here to the front line to direct you."

"You are doin' a fine job of that, sir," Cole said.

"Maybe you need to try a different spot," Ballard said. "Maybe he's not here."

"Where the hell would he be? Back in Beijing?" Cole snapped. "Sir. I don't reckon we're that lucky. You just got to accept that he ain't never gonna do what you want him to."

"Dammit, Cole." Ballard looked at the reporter. "Don't put any of that last part in the newspaper, you hear?"

"Got it, sir," Hardy replied, who paused scribbling in his notepad.

"What are you doing out here, sir?" Cole wondered. "If you want to help me, you'll get the hell out of here."

"Don't tell me where I should be, goddammit," Ballard retorted. When Cole didn't respond, he added, "Got it?"

"Have it your way, sir."

An uneasy silence settled over the trench. Most men wouldn't have dared to talk to an officer that way, but Cole didn't give a damn. Ballard stewed over that for a minute.

To the reporter's credit, he wore an abashed look on his face, as if he might be aware that he and Ballard were just getting in the way.

"Go ahead and ask him some questions," Ballard said. "Then you can take our picture again."

"Sure thing, Lieutenant." The reporter flipped to a fresh page in his notebook, which he proceeded to drop in the mud. Cursing, he picked it up and flipped it open to yet another page. "OK, what are you looking for out there?"

Cole thought about telling him that he was looking for a place to shove that pencil and notebook, but he noticed Ballard waiting for an answer.

"Any bit of movement," Cole replied. "The best thing to do is kind of stare through the scope and not focus on anything. Just let your eye pass over it. Any little flicker, anything out of the ordinary, it catches your eye."

The reporter leaned closer, obviously interested. "Then what?"

"Then you stare hard at it. Try to see what caught your attention. Sooner or later, if it is anything, you'll know."

"Huh," the reporter said, scribbling down Cole's words. Cole found it to be a strange sensation that someone would bother to write down something that he said. The less he said in that case, the better. He clammed up, wishing that Ballard and the reporter would go away.

However, the reporter didn't seem to be through with him yet, although he seemed to sense Cole's reticence. "Just one more question," he said. "What's the number one rule of being a sniper?"

Cole couldn't help but grin. He snorted. "Don't get shot, or better yet, 'Shoot the other guy first.'"

The reporter jotted that down, but kept the pencil poised over his notebook, as if expecting more. Like maybe a real answer. "Anything else?" he prompted.

"Let me tell you something now. Write this down in your little book there. War is a lot of things. It ain't just fightin'. It's making your enemy cold and afraid, cutting off his supplies, making him keep his head down all the time, making him think that, you know what, maybe his whole way of life ain't the right one. Make him reconsider his choices. That's what I am doing here, one bullet at a time."

The reporter took a long time getting every word of that down. Meanwhile, Ballard was staring at Cole. "I thought you were just another dumb cracker," he muttered.

"I reckon most of us see what we want to see, sir," Cole said. "A smart man sees what is."

The lieutenant didn't have an answer to that.

Having finished with his notebook, the reporter tucked it away and raised his camera instead. He took three or four photos of the three other men, posed in positions with the kid on the binoculars, Cole on the rifle, and Ballard touching Cole's shoulder and pointing.

"We're done here," the lieutenant announced. "I need to get Hardy out of here so he can send his film back and write that article."

"Yes, sir."

The lieutenant and the reporter scrambled back out of the hole, keeping low. Cole wasn't sorry to see them go.

But their going also revealed a truth that Cole still hadn't nailed that enemy sniper. All that he had done was talk about it, which made him feel cheap and hollow.

Why was it that talking about anything seemed to spoil it? Better to keep it to yourself.

Another hour passed. The sun climbed higher. Cole's scalp started to itch, so he took off his helmet. It was easier to get up close to the wall of the trench without it, anyway.

He had the kid waggle the helmet on a stick, but nothing doing. The other sniper didn't take a shot.

The kid dug some rations out of his haversack and shared them with Cole. They washed it down with a few gulps from their canteens.

It had gotten so quiet on the front line that a soldier a hundred yards away made the mistake of raising his head out of his foxhole, thinking to take a better look at the Chinese on the opposite ridge. Seconds later, a bullet came in and killed him. The sound of the rifle shot followed, echoing across the ridges and valley.

Wherever the Chinese sniper had been, he was back now.

"The shot came from off to the left," the kid said, trying desperately to see anything over there.

Cole knew that he wouldn't see any sign of the sniper. The sniper would be well hidden, just as Cole was here. They would only catch a glimpse of him if they were very, very lucky.

Something that stood out was how far off that shot had been. The echo of the rifle shot had sounded different than how it had yesterday. Same sector, but a different spot. One thing for sure, the sniper was a long way off.

There was no point in trying the helmet on a stick trick again. He had not fallen for it yesterday. Then again, why not?

"Kid, here's what I want you to do." Cole nodded at his helmet. "Go ahead and put my helmet on a stick and raise it above the trench. Let's see what happens. Maybe he'll take the bait."

The kid did as he was told, and Cole waited, tense behind the rifle scope, hoping to catch a glimpse of a muzzle flash or some other tiny sign of where the sniper lay hidden. When the enemy fired, he couldn't miss it.

Nothing happened. The kid raised the helmet and waved it back and forth, like a flag in front of a bull. Still nothing.

"Never mind, kid. Put your helmet back on."

"Guess he's not interested," the kid said. He picked up the binoculars again. "Hold on. That wasn't there before. Do you see that off to the left?"

"What?"

"It's a ... I think it's a bottle."

CHAPTER EIGHTEEN

CHEN HAD BEEN in position since before dawn, making his way into the Chinese line in the darkness. By now he knew this route by memory because he had passed down this path so many times before. The weather was still warm enough to wear the soft-soled shoes that he preferred, and this enabled him to move almost silently in the gray pre-dawn light.

He felt like a true soldier, moving with the stealth of a lion, just as his fellow Chinese warriors had done for centuries. Instead of a spear, he carried a rifle.

Every soldier and peasant knew that it was best to go quietly in the dark, rather than awaken the enemies and predators that lurked in the night.

The quiet moment was broken only by a grunt and the sound of stumbling footsteps, reminding him that he was not alone. Once again, accompanying him this morning was Major Wu.

Chen paused and asked, "Are you all right, sir?"

"Fine, fine," Wu said, ending with a chuckle. "Not all of us have your eagle eyes, you know."

Wu had traveled even lighter than usual, not even bothering with a rifle. Instead, he wore a holster on his belt. A pair of binoculars was slung around his neck. He had brought along a small rucksack with some cold rice and dried fish, which he shared with Chen when they paused on their hike up Sniper Ridge.

"We cannot have our sniper going hungry," Wu said. "Dried fish for you. Only the best!"

Chen ate, cognizant of the fact that the food, though barely more than peasant fare, was far better than what any of the troops were eating this morning.

The major had also brought along a bottle of rice wine, but Chen took only a few measured sips just to chase away the morning chill and wash down the food. He would have preferred tea.

Wu drank enough for both of them.

Even in the dim light, Chen could see that characteristically, Wu had worn his political officer's uniform that looked so out of place in the outdoorsy surroundings, like he was headed for a dress parade. Not for the first time, Chen was reminded of a barnyard peacock, right down to Wu's noisy strut down the path—when he was not stumbling over his own two feet and making enough noise for a company of water buffalo.

They moved into position as the light slowly grew over the eastern hills, illuminating the landscape before them. The scenery was steep and forbidding, but by now, the harsh hills and mountains surrounding them seemed like old friends.

Chen studied the defenses nearby, then the valley before them, and finally the hilltop opposite them where the American and UN troops awaited dawn while crouched in their own defenses. Of course, Chen couldn't actually see the enemy soldiers, but he sensed that they were there.

As the light grew, one of the enemy soldiers grew careless, heaving himself out of a foxhole and walking along the ridge toward another position. He didn't seem to be in any particular hurry or sense that he was in grave danger. Normally, he would have been fine. He was too distant for the Chinese soldiers to be any threat. What the soldier had not counted on was Chen's presence.

Chen followed the soldier in his telescopic sight, leading him slightly, before pulling the trigger and putting an end to him. One moment the man was living; the next he was not.

A lesson for us all, Chen thought. He slid the bolt back and forth, readying another round.

Wu grunted in approval. He watched nearby through the binoculars. "The first one of the day," he said, then paused to raise the bottle it in a toast. He seemed intent on drinking most of the bottle during the course of the morning. "Here's to many more."

Activity on the other side had slowed, however, because word had gotten out about the sniper. In any case, that was Chen's suspicion. Even the Americans were fools only to a point.

He was curious about the fact that an American sniper had opposed him yesterday. He had gotten lucky with a shot that he thought had hit the enemy sniper's spotter. Someone over there had the same job that Wu had on this side.

Even if Chen had not killed the spotter, then he had certainly wounded him. However, he was sure that the enemy sniper had gone unscathed. Some of the enemy's shots had struck close to his own position, which gave Chen pause.

First of all, it was a very long distance to shoot so accurately. He felt challenged by the distance. Somehow, the enemy sniper was able to shoot almost as well. Although he had been guessing at Chen's position, he had come unerringly close

The problem for both snipers was that neither man could see the other. Both of them were so well buried into their sniper's nests that there was very little chance of either man presenting himself as a target to the other one. The other man's spotter had made the mistake of letting himself be seen by Chen. Just a glimpse, but it had been enough.

Chen had the unpatriotic thought that perhaps he could rid himself of Wu in much the same way if the opportunity presented itself. He had already lost one spotter at the Chosin Reservoir, but losing Wu was something of a double-edged sword, however. As pushy as Wu could be, he had also become Chen's champion. Who would save him a place at the fire, if not Wu?

"Please keep your head down, sir," Chen said.

"Surely, none of them can shoot that far." Wu laughed, then seemed to reconsider and did what Chen suggested, keeping his head down. "Then again, maybe they can. You would know best."

But as it grew lighter, Major Wu sipped his wine and seemed to grow bored.

"What are you waiting for?" Wu asked. "Go ahead and shoot a few more of them. We must strike fear into the hearts of the imperialists as always. Sitting here quietly achieves nothing."

Glancing over at the commissar, he saw that Wu wore a grin on his face, but Chen knew better than to mistake that smile for lightheartedness. No, Major Wu was deadly serious.

"For too long, the Chinese have been victimized by the imperialist nations," Wu said. "Now, Chinese warriors are on the move again to reclaim the respect that has been lost. We will push these invaders back into the sea."

Chen himself would have liked nothing better, and he silently agreed that Wu was right on several counts. The Chinese had a proud and rich heritage, but their culture in the previous two centuries had not kept pace with the innovations of the west. This insularity had put them at a disadvantage that enabled the western nations to exploit the Chinese. After the war had upset the world order, the trend of exploitation had finally come to an end with the rise of Chairman Mao and Chinese communism. This was a new way forward for their nation and people.

"The enemy is weak," Chen agreed.

"Never forget what we have lost and endured," Wu said. "Never forget that there is only one way forward for our people."

It was quite a speech, and wasted on Chen, who was a man of simple beliefs. In his mind, the enemy soldiers were like wild dogs trying to snatch away whatever scraps they could. Perhaps the major had spoken those words for his own benefit, rather than Chen's. Maybe it was the rice wine talking.

"Never benefit oneself; only benefit others," Chen said, repeating a popular Communist Chinese slogan that had been drummed into him, only because the speech seemed to warrant some acknowledgment.

"Good, good, very good. Come, Comrade Sniper," Wu said, grinning. "Carve out your place in history."

"If you see any targets, please let me know, Comrade Major," Chen said, pointedly. After all, it was Wu's job to be the spotter. Pretty speeches were not enough.

"You are right, of course," Wu agreed, making one of his amused chuckles, and brought the binoculars to his eyes. He scanned the American lines looking for any sign of movement.

Half an hour went by before Wu snapped, "There on the right!"

Chen swung the rifle in that direction, although *swung* wasn't the right definition. It was more that he adjusted the rifle a fraction until he saw the American soldier in his crosshairs.

The man had foolishly put his head above the rim of his foxhole. He was much too far away for Chen to see his face, much less read his facial expression, but he seemed to be staring out into the promise of the day. For him, the day would be short-lived.

Chen's finger took up tension on the trigger until the rifle bucked against his shoulder and hundreds of feet in the distance, the soldier crumpled into his foxhole.

Chen tensed, wondering if there would be an answering shot. If the American sniper was in his trench on the opposite side, then he would now know that Chen was plying his own trade and the other man would be hunting for him, just as Chen was now doing.

More time passed; the sun grew higher. Chen had a peasant's natural affinity for the weather and the sun was a welcome relief from the gloom that they had experienced for several days on end. Briefly, he took his face away from the rifle and turned it toward the sun. The sun even held a bit of warmth as if it had kept something back from the summer, but wanted to use it all up before winter arrived.

Overhead, the enemy planes soared and occasionally dropped their bombs and napalm on more distant sections of the ridge or more remote hills. So far, the American planes had not come close to where Chen and Wu lay hidden.

"I see something," Wu said after awhile. "It is a helmet."

Through the scope, Chen spotted the helmet, just visible over the rim of the trench. Frustratingly, a face did not reveal itself beneath the helmet. The helmet bobbed a bit in the way that a fisherman jiggles the bait.

"A trick," Chen said.

He looked more closely. *What was that?* He stared into the scope. Although the distance was great, he could see some sort of mark on the front of the helmet. He felt a mental flicker of recognition. Even at this distance, he thought that it might be the flag that decorated the American sniper's helmet. The sniper that he had faced before. In spite of himself, Chen's breath quickened.

He had no doubt now that this was the sniper that he had dueled with yesterday. To his surprise, it even seemed to be the same location. This seemed to be arrogance on the enemy sniper's part—or perhaps foolishness.

"Are you going to fire?" Wu wondered.

"No."

After a minute, the helmet sank out of sight. But Chen now knew where the sniper was hidden, even if he could not see him directly. His eye never wavered from that magnified circle in the rifle scope, in hopes that he might catch a glimpse of a target. All that he needed was a second, a moment, in which to pull the trigger. That was all that he had needed yesterday to shoot the spotter. Would he be so lucky again?

Occasionally, artillery exchanged fire, but the firing was desultory. Again, Major Wu seemed to grow bored. He was a man built for movement and not one to bide his time.

By now, he had drunk up all the wine, with Chen having just a few sips.

"That is the end of that," Wu said, giving the bottle a shake. "Where is that enemy sniper? I know a way to draw him out, which is why I have emptied this bottle for you."

"What way?" Chen wondered.

He realized from the careful way that Major Wu spoke that the political officer might be somewhat intoxicated.

Wu's next actions proved Chen's suspicions. The major took the empty wine bottle and placed it on top of a rock beside their hiding place, in plain sight.

"What are you doing?" Chen asked anxiously.

"Enough of these games," Wu said. "We need to show the enemy sniper where we are hidden so that he will fire at us and then you can return fire and finish him off."

That is a terrible idea, Chen thought. However, what he said was, "What an excellent idea, sir."

"Yes, yes, we've agreed. Now, keep your head down and let's see what happens."

But no shots came right away.

"I don't understand," Wu said, putting the binoculars back to his eyes and scanning the opposite ridge. Suddenly, he paused and murmured, "Wait, I don't believe it."

Through the scope, Chen saw at once what had caused Wu's astonishment.

"The Americans have done the same thing," Wu said. "They have placed, not a bottle, but maybe one of their canteens on a rock on their side."

One moment the object had not been there, and then it had. Chen wondered what it all meant. Was it a trick? Here was the bottle on their side, and the Americans had set up a canteen on their side.

He sensed that a gauntlet had been tossed down. Should Chen pick it up? He pressed his eye more tightly against the scope, searching for any movement on the American side, feeling the metal ring digging into the soft flesh.

"This is interesting," Wu said. "But what does it mean? Is it a signal of some sort?"

They did not have to wait long to find out. Moments later, a bullet struck the base of the rock that held the bottle. Fragments of rock flew, one of them even stinging Wu's face and drawing blood. Wu swore in a distinctly non-Maoist fashion.

Chen considered that the enemy's aim could have been better because the other marksman hadn't managed to hit the political officer or the bottle.

Another bullet came in, striking even closer, but again, sparing the bottle and Wu, who was keeping his head down.

After a glance at Wu, who was swiping at his injured face with a handkerchief, Chen went back to his rifle scope. He knew that he was well hidden in his own sniper's den. It would take the eyes of a hawk to catch a glimpse of his camouflaged rifle muzzle or to detect the glassy glint of his telescopic sight. He worked in relative safety. With that knowledge, he decided that if it was a game that the other sniper wanted, then it was a game that he would get.

He looked through the scope to just where the canteen was sitting in plain view on the American side.

As he looked, another shot struck near the bottle sitting just a couple of feet from Chen's position. Try as he might, he could not see the other sniper. The man was just as well hidden as Chen himself.

Here was someone who knew his craft, but Chen was not discouraged. Looking through the sight at the canteen, he decided to take a shot at it. The American could not hit the bottle, but perhaps Chen could hit the canteen. This was the game that they would play as snipers.

He held the crosshairs a little bit above and to the right of the canteen, accounting for distance and the slight breeze. His finger began to take up tension on the trigger. He held his breath and ever so slowly, his finger took up the last bit of tension. The rifle fired.

A full second later, the canteen flew off the rock and disappeared.

Beside him in the sniper's hide, Major Wu had been watching through binoculars. The officer laughed happily at the sight of the canteen flying away.

Chen allowed himself a rare smile.

Whatever game he and the other sniper were playing at, Chen suspected that he had just won.

CHAPTER NINETEEN

THROUGH THE SCOPE, Cole could clearly see the bottle that had been placed on a rock over on the Chinese side. It was so far away that with the naked eye, it would be less than a speck. But someone who was looking, such as a sniper like Cole, would have known immediately that something in the landscape had changed and that the bottle had suddenly appeared.

Who over there was taunting them? It could have been any soldier, but he doubted that because the bottle had been placed just where he suspected that the Chinese sniper was hidden.

"Don't that beat all," Cole muttered. "Kid, you got your canteen handy?"

"Yeah," the kid said. "Why? You thirsty?"

"Nope. What I want you to do is take your canteen and stick it on that rock just on the other side of this here hole we're in. Be quick about it," he warned. "Keep your head down. I don't want you to get shot in the process."

"All right," the kid said, sounding mystified, not knowing what Cole had in mind. "Is this because of the bottle on the other side?"

"Yep," Cole said. "We're gonna have us an old-fashioned turkey shoot."

From the kid's blank look, it was clear that he had no idea what Cole was talking about. "Turkey shoot?"

"Shooting contest," Cole explained. "You know, when I was a boy, there was a famous one that took place between my pa and another bootlegger. Leastways, it was famous in our neck of the woods. Maybe you'd call it infamous."

"What happened?"

"Well now, my pa and this other bootlegger got to arguin' over who was the better shot. They was both known for being handy with a rifle. They had the idea to have themselves a shooting contest to settle that argument for once and for all. Trouble was, they had to find a time when they were both sober enough to hit anything."

"Yeah?" The kid's tone indicated that he was wondering where this story was going. "What were they shooting for? Was there some kind of prize? Like they won a turkey?"

"They bet each other a dollar, but you could say the stakes was higher than that. You see, whoever won was the better shot. They ain't no bigger stakes than that where I come from."

"I've got a feeling that the stakes are plenty big here, too," the kid said. "Like the loser might get shot."

"Go on now. Set that canteen out and be quick about it."

The kid did as Cole had told him to do. Quickly, he placed the canteen on a rock, then got back down into the trench.

Cole was already lining up the shot with his eye pressed to the rifle scope, aiming carefully at the target in the distance. Even through the scope, he had to admit that the bottle was not much of a target. Damn small at this distance. But like his pa, Cole reckoned that he had something to prove. The stakes here were every bit as high as they had been between his pa and that rival bootlegger.

He took in a breath, let it out, took in another, exhaled it. Slowly, slowly his finger caressed the trigger. Some part of his brain calculated where to aim by instinct.

The rifle fired.

He continued gazing through the scope, fully expecting the bottle to shatter. A second passed, then another, but the bottle still stood.

Damn it all, he thought, without letting himself get rattled. He worked the bolt, inserted another shell, and aimed again at the distant bottle, a little higher this time and to the left, to account for the slight breeze.

Once again, he put gentle tension on the trigger, waited until the puff of wind had died, and took up the last bit of tension so that the rifle fired.

"You missed," said the kid helpfully.

"No shit," Cole muttered, then worked the bolt again. *Third time gonna be the charm,* he thought. At least, he sure as hell hoped so.

Again, he lined up the crosshairs on the bottle in the distance and aimed carefully.

He was sure that their own hiding place was beyond the prying eyes of the enemy sniper, although he would certainly be able to narrow it down now that Cole had fired twice. Also, there was the fact that they now had a canteen marking their position. It was all foolish, he thought. But he couldn't resist taking another crack at that bottle.

Putting all other thoughts out of his mind, Cole slowly squeezed the trigger until the rifle fired again. He watched through the scope, willing the bullet to strike true.

Again, a second passed and then another.

The bottle stood just where it had been, untouched.

"Damn," Cole muttered.

Then a bullet came in and hit the canteen dead center so that it went flying over their heads and down into the trench.

The kid picked up the canteen and stuck a finger in the bullet hole. Water leaked out everywhere and joined the mud at the bottom of the trench.

"He sure killed that canteen," the kid said.

Cole reloaded the rifle but didn't bother to take another shot at the bottle. He was beginning to get the feeling that he might shoot at it all day and not hit the damn thing. What the hell was wrong with him?

He had the sinking feeling that just maybe the Chinese sniper was a better shot.

All along the trenches and foxholes, it had been fairly quiet for a while, so the little flurry of shooting between the two sides had drawn some attention and broken up the monotony.

Off to the left, about a hundred feet down from Cole's position, some poor soldier was a little too curious and raised his head higher out of his foxhole than was prudent. There was another shot from the Chinese side.

Cole heard screams from the wounded man and more shouts for a medic. Then finally, ominously, the screaming ended and only a few bitter curses were coming from that direction.

The Chinese sniper had proved himself deadly yet again, and Cole had been unable to stop him.

He had out-gunned Cole and then he had killed another soldier. Cole slumped down into the trench, feeling defeated. This was the same sniper who had wounded Pomeroy yesterday. Instead of getting even with the enemy sniper, Cole had allowed the man to show him up. It didn't sit right with Cole, that was for damn sure.

Winking at him in the afternoon sunlight, the bottle still stood near the enemy sniper's position.

Finally, the shadows of the day lengthened. The sun went behind the mountains and all the warmth was sucked out of the day as a reminder that another Korean winter was just around the corner. Stars began to glitter faintly on the horizon and the nighttime cold came down.

"Time to head back, kid," Cole announced.

He hadn't so much as taken another shot the rest of the day. The truth was that his heart just hadn't been in it. Not that many targets had presented themselves. The enemy soldiers had sense enough to keep out of sight.

Now that it was dark enough to move under cover of night, he and the kid slipped out of the trench and began to make their way back toward headquarters.

"It wasn't such a good day, was it?" the kid said.

"I reckon not," Cole said.

"There's always tomorrow," the kid added, but Cole didn't answer. They hiked the rest of the way down from the ridge in silence. Once they had reached the camp, Cole sent the kid off to the mess tent to get himself something to eat. He had one more stop to make first, and truth be told, Cole needed some time alone just to think.

He slung his rifle over his shoulder and headed in the direction of the field hospital. On the way, he wondered if maybe he had lost his touch with the rifle.

Because you couldn't hit a bottle? Who gives a damn? But the other fella didn't seem to have that problem. Cole shook his head and walked on.

He had hoped to find Pomeroy that evening and tell him that he had bumped off the enemy sniper and gotten even. Unfortunately, that wasn't the case, but Cole still owed Pomeroy a visit. Hell, he had gotten shot helping Cole. It was the least that he could do.

He pushed through the tent flaps and walked into the oppressive smell that all field hospitals have, a medley of alcohol and urine, and the vague sweetness of rotting meat. Cole tried to tell himself that there were worse places to be—like maybe hell itself.

He walked on down the rows, shaking his head at how many wounded there were, bandaged and beat to hell in just about every way, shape, and form imaginable. The wounded just seemed to keep piling up steadily day after day.

He reckoned that's what happened when you had two armies trading hilltops. The wounded tended to stack up, along with the dead. And for what? Some godforsaken hill? Cole tried not to think too much about the answer. He hadn't invented war and he supposed that it never made a whole lot of sense in the end.

After a while, walking up and down the rows of wounded, Cole realized that he couldn't find Pomeroy. He seemed to have the right row of hospital beds, but his old friend was nowhere to be found. Maybe there had been some sort of mix-up or Cole just hadn't remembered right. After all, if you'd seen one hospital cot, you'd kind of seen them all.

Finally, Cole tracked down an orderly and approached him. "Say buddy," he drawled, "I'm lookin' for a friend of mine. He was right here just yesterday."

"What was his name?" the orderly asked.

Cole told him and the orderly checked a chart.

"Pomeroy ... Oh yeah, he got evacuated today," the orderly said. "Your friend is a lucky bastard. He's probably on a plane to Tokyo by now."

"You mean he's gone?"

"Yep, that's about the size of it," the orderly said. "Unfortunately, we've got plenty of others to take his place."

"Lucky bastard," Cole echoed faintly and then retreated from the field hospital.

Outside, glad of the fresh air, the realization struck him like a blow that he was unlikely ever to see Pomeroy again. He hadn't had a chance to say his goodbyes, not realizing that he wouldn't get the opportunity. Cole had thought that being shown up by the Chinese sniper was the worst thing that had happened to him today, but the news that Pomeroy had been flown out without a proper farewell was a close second. It just didn't set right with him.

Walking back through the camp, Cole felt like a kicked dog.

CHAPTER TWENTY

COLE SPOTTED Lieutenant Ballard and ducked his head, hoping to avoid giving a run-down of what had happened up on the ridge. Once he heard how Cole had screwed up and let the enemy get the best of him, Ballard just might put him back to washing dishes and peeling potatoes.

He had planned to pay a visit to the mess tent to see what he could scrounge up in the way of hot food, but now he wasn't so hungry.

Instead of the mess area, he headed off to find the pup tent that he shared with the kid, in hopes of getting some sleep. Suddenly, he felt deeply exhausted. He didn't even bother to clean his rifle, which he usually did the way that some men said their prayers at night.

He had never been so down. It wasn't in his nature to admit defeat, but it hadn't been an easy couple of days. First, he had seen those American soldiers killed by the Chinese sniper and then he had lost a shooting match, which wounded his pride deeply. He had also lost Pomeroy. Cole took some comfort in the fact that the SOB was still alive and on a plane away from the fighting, but it was unlikely that Cole would see his old friend again anytime soon.

He crawled into the pup tent and found that the kid was already there, fast asleep, after having hit the mess tent. The kid stirred just long enough to open one eyelid at Cole's arrival.

"There you are," he said. "Lieutenant Ballard was looking for you."

"What the hell did he want?"

"Didn't say," the kid said. "And I didn't ask. I was too busy eating at the time, but I thought that I'd pass along the message."

He rolled over and promptly fell back asleep.

Cole had no idea what Ballard could have wanted with him, but he was sure that it wasn't good. His stomach had rumbled at the mention of food, but he welcomed the pang of hunger. It took him back to his boyhood, and all the nights that he had lain awake, hungry in the dark, before heading out to hunt in the morning.

There was nothing like hunger pangs to motivate you. How many times had he gone into the woods with no more than a single bullet or shotgun shell because that was all there was to spare. Somehow, he had almost always managed to come back with something to help feed his family while his pa was on a bender or off in the hills, cooking his shine.

There had been a cloak of responsibility weighing on his young shoulders to provide for his ma and his brothers and sisters. But it had also been a point of pride that he could help fill their bellies.

His thoughts wandering now, Cole realized that he probably wasn't going to fall asleep, tired though he was. Enviously, he listened to the even breathing that the kid made beside him. Whatever happened in the days ahead, he had to make sure that the kid survived. Hell, he owed him that much. After all, being Cole's spotter was starting to get dangerous.

The kid had mentioned trying for the enemy sniper again tomorrow, but Cole wasn't so sure about that. He was already down. How many times did he want to get kicked?

Not wanting to toss and turn and wake the kid, he took his blanket and carried it outside. He wanted to glimpse the stars in the night sky.

It was a clear, crisp autumn night and somewhere riding the breeze, he could smell wood smoke from some soldier's campfire. He wasn't sure if it came from the American side or from the Chinese side, but no matter; it was a comforting smell all the same.

He looked up at the sky and saw the glittering pinpricks of the stars. His father had taught him the constellations as a boy and even here in the sky of Korea, he could recognize some of them. There was Cassiopeia, in all her mythic beauty, and also low on the horizon crouched Orion, the Hunter, recognizable by the three stars in a row that made up his belt.

A hunter in the sky and one below watching him. Cole took that to be a good omen.

Nonetheless, it took a long time for sleep to find him.

It was only after he pulled his rifle closer, smelling the familiar gunpowder and the gun oil, that he was finally able to sleep.

* * *

IN THE MORNING, the squad was rotated out for sentry duty and Cole joined them rather than return to the ridge to face the enemy sniper again.

Their role was to guard the main road leading to the base, but it was a cakewalk in that they didn't have to worry any about the enemy. The Chinese were all in the hills and mountains, but not on the open plain that led nearly twenty miles back to Seoul.

Cole carried his scoped Springfield on a sling over one shoulder. Although he wouldn't be needing it down here on sentry duty, it wasn't safe to leave the rifle in his tent for somebody from another unit to "requisition" something as scarce as a sniper rifle. In this Army, possession was nine-tenths of the law.

It was dull duty, but it was a hell of a lot better than being up on the line getting shot at. The platoon was rotated in and out of sentry duty to give the soldiers a break. In addition, every few days they had a day in camp just to clean and inspect their equipment. Mostly, they used that down time just to smoke cigarettes, play cards, write letters home, and sleep. Soldiers never could get enough sleep.

Right now, at the southern entrance to the encampment, the most that they had to worry about were officers coming and going. And even they weren't all that important, because the officers who mattered came and went by helicopter, not Jeep. This morning, however, the road into and out of camp seemed particularly busy, with the tough Jeeps churning through the muddy roads. Several trucks arrived, laden with ammo or reinforcements, most of whom wore spanking new uniforms.

"Look at all those greenbeans. More fodder for the cannons," said one of the sentries, shaking his head.

"Something's up," the kid said. "Lots of traffic."

"Maybe there's another attack planned," Cole said. "The Chinese still hold Sniper Ridge, and I know that doesn't sit well with the brass."

"You're probably right," the kid agreed. "But when that attack happens, I hope that I'm back here on sentry duty."

Ballard approached, and Cole tensed. He hadn't seen the lieutenant since the kid's warning last night that Ballard was looking for him.

Now, the lieutenant had found him.

"Cole, goddammit, where have you been?"

"Sir? I—"

"Never mind," Ballard said impatiently. "Listen up. You have got to do something about that sniper up there on the ridge. Everybody from the colonel on down has been on me about it."

"You, sir?"

"Yes, me. Because I have the unfortunate situation of having you in my platoon, and word has gotten around that you are the best shot we've got. Which puts me in charge of snipers and counter-sniper measures, apparently. All of which I need like I need a hole in the head."

"If you say so, sir."

Ballard glared at him. "If you were an actual sniper, you'd be getting the job done and we wouldn't have that problem with that Chinese dead-eye, now would we?"

Cole glared at the lieutenant, but had the good sense to tamp down what he really wanted to say. "No sir, I reckon not."

"Think about that, Cole. Think about how you can eliminate him."

"Yes, sir."

"You'll get your chance tomorrow," Ballard added. "There's going to be another attack on Sniper Ridge. We are going to take it back from the enemy for good."

Ballard stalked off, grumbling, and leaving a silent Cole in his wake.

They went back to guard duty, watching the comings and goings of Jeeps and trucks, but that was mostly quiet—a little too quiet. Cole never had a whole lot to say, and they were all feeling the absence from the squad of the loquacious Pomeroy, but the hillbilly marksman was especially silent this morning.

The kid couldn't help but start jabbering to fill the quiet. "I sure do miss Pomeroy," the kid said. "At least he had something to say now and then."

"I reckon we all miss him, kid."

"Why didn't you go back to that ridge this morning, Cole?" the kid asked. He was always cautious about calling Cole "hillbilly" like Pomeroy had. "I would have gone with you."

"I don't know," Cole said. "Maybe I needed to take a break."

"By coming down here and watching the brass go by in their Jeeps?" The kid paused. "Wait a minute. You're not *scared*, are you?"

Cole bristled. "Scared of what?"

"Well, you missed that Chinese sniper yesterday and when you got into that shooting contest, you couldn't seem to hit that old bottle that the enemy stuck out there on a rock. The other guy didn't seem to have any trouble hitting our canteen."

"Thanks a lot for noticing, kid," Cole said, tamping down his anger because he knew that the kid was just stating the obvious. "Ballard already busted my balls about all this, and the last thing I need is more of the same from you."

For now, it appeared that the lieutenant was keeping him on sniper duty. He was sure that the lieutenant would have taken away the scoped rifle and given it to someone else if there had been any good candidates. At the same time, Cole also felt a weight on his shoulders. The kid's comments were not helping.

Cole held out the rifle to the kid. "Kid, do you think maybe you want to give it a try and see if you can do any better?"

The kid stared at him and shook his head. "I don't know what's gotten into you, but I can sure tell you one thing. Nobody else can shoot like you can, Cole."

"Listen, kid—"

"No, let me finish," the kid said. "You have got to be the coolest customer with a rifle that I've ever seen. That anybody has seen. You were born to do this, Cole. I'm not like you. None of us is like you. This is what you were made for."

"In case you didn't notice, I almost got Pomeroy killed."

"If Pomeroy were here, he would agree with me. So what, you had a bad day. Your one bad day is better than any of the rest of us could do in a year."

Having said his piece, the kid turned and walked away, giving Cole something to chew over.

The lieutenant had kicked him in the ass a short while ago. That, he could take. The kid had just kicked him in the gut, which hurt a whole lot worse.

Having walked a few feet away, the kid stopped and looked back at Cole.

"What are you still doing here?" the kid asked. "You need to get after that sniper."

For the first time in a while, Cole grinned. But there was nothing humorous or friendly in his expression. It was more like a wolf showing its teeth.

Nervously, the kid took a step back, as if to create some distance between them.

"All right, kid," Cole said. "You win."

He left the guard post and started to walk back toward the main encampment.

"Hey, where are you going?" the kid called after him.

Cole said over his shoulder, "If you see the lieutenant, tell him I went hunting."

CHAPTER TWENTY-ONE

COLE KNEW that he had to get his mind right if he was going to have a chance at getting this enemy sniper for once and for all, and that started with getting his rifle right.

It was time to return to the basics.

What nagged at him from yesterday's shooting match was that he *should* have hit the target. It wasn't like him to miss anything that he shot at. Well, not miss all that much, at any rate. He especially did not to miss three times in a row, like he had missed that bottle. His sights had been just where they should have been. He had not jerked the trigger or coughed at the last instant, sending the bullet astray.

What if it hadn't been him, but the rifle itself?

There was only one thing to do to find that out, which was to put the rifle through its paces.

Cole went out to the edges of the camp, out to where the plain opened up, away from the hills and ridges where the fighting was taking place. He had stopped by the mess area and procured a couple of empty bottles, not so different from the ones that he'd been shooting at unsuccessfully the day before. He set one of the bottles on a rock and walked back about a hundred yards and then put his rifle across another rock, his rolled-up jacket underneath the stock.

One thing about Korea, he thought, was that there wasn't any shortage of rocks.

He recalled that another soldier who'd had some geology classes had said that these were rocks were mostly something called Jurassic granite, formed into mountains millions of years ago by the collision of the Chinese landmass against the Korean peninsula. Something prophetic there, he reckoned.

Cole laid his hand on the boulder for a moment, trying to imagine the violent forces that had brought it here. It was kind of hard to wrap his head around the concept of millions of years, although it made his own struggles seem puny by comparison.

What had come before the rocks and mountains? Maybe just God himself?

Cole shook his head. *I'm just a spark*, he reminded himself. *Just a muzzle flash*. The thought was both humbling and reassuring.

Before his musings got too deep in the weeds, he got back to the business at hand. He studied the bottle, which was a lot closer than the one that he had shot at—and missed—just yesterday.

He put his eye to the scope and his target sprang much closer, considering that the scope was sited in for this distance. All that he should have to do was to put his crosshairs on the target and then watch as the bottle shattered.

Cole smirked. The *idea* of shooting was the simplest thing in the world. What's so hard about pointing and aiming, right? However, actually hitting what you were pointing at could turn out to be one of the hardest things in the world.

Slowly, he let his finger take up tension on the trigger until the rifle fired.

Through the scope, he was surprised to see that the bottle was still standing. This was like yesterday all over again. Curious now, he worked the bolt and put another shell into the chamber. He then lined up the crosshairs once again and squeezed off another round.

The bottle was still standing. There was a slope behind the bottle, and he had seen the bullet raise a puff of dust as it hit a little high and to the right.

He adjusted the scope, then he lined up the sights again right at the shoulder of the bottle.

Thanks to that ancient boulder that the rifle was resting upon, his aim was literally rock solid.

He squeezed the trigger.

This time, the bottle shattered into a hundred pieces as the bullet struck true.

Huh. At that moment, realization flooded through him and he felt foolish. It wasn't that his aim had been off or that he had flinched at the last minute, but that he had made a different kind of mistake.

Maybe the worst kind.

He had simply thought that the rifle was sighted in, when in reality the telescopic sight was a little off. The telescopic site was a wonder compared to iron sights and it enabled him to hit just about anything he could see. But only if it was properly sighted in.

The optical sight was finicky. It didn't take much jostling to throw the scope off, and that must've been what happened. It could have happened when he jumped down into the ditch. It could have happened when the rifle was jarred at some point when he didn't notice. Maybe even the contraction of going from cool autumn mornings to warm afternoon sun had moved something out of alignment.

How it had happened was less important than the simple truth that the sight hadn't been lined up accurately.

He went down and put another bottle on the rock, then walked back to his old spot and fired off another round just to double check.

Once again, the bottle shattered.

Cole grinned, feeling an energetic warmth spread through him that he hadn't felt in a while.

The next step in Cole's plan gradually started to take shape about how he was going to bag this enemy sniper for once and for all.

Deep down inside him, the part of himself that he called the critter was waking up. He could feel that cold, killing part of him flexing its claws, gnashing its fangs, sniffing the air. The critter was hungry.

Next, he had to know where to do his hunting.

* * *

IT WAS no secret that the Chinese constantly infiltrated the camp, usually at night. Small squads cut communications wires, set fires, even blew up trucks using hand grenades—and then melted back into the darkness.

For the American troops, these enemy raids were a constant source of uneasiness, not to mention frustration. The question was, how did the raiders manage to come and go unseen?

He'd overheard Ballard complaining again that very morning about how a group of Chinese raiders come behind enemy lines and caused trouble. They had lobbed a couple of grenades into trucks, turning them into burning hulks, and generally raised hell.

These incursions didn't have much strategic value, but served as a reminder that small numbers of the enemy could come and go seemingly at will.

Cole wondered about that. How had those Chinese managed yet again to slip right through the American lines? Clearly, they weren't coming through the very center of the line across from Sniper Ridge. That way was too heavily defended, covered by machine guns and artillery, and troops.

Hell, a mouse could hardly get through the center of the line without catching a bullet. No, he thought, the entry point must be somewhere along the flanks. That was the only explanation for how the Chinese were getting through.

As someone who had been in places where no one wanted him to be, Cole had a theory or two about where the enemy was infiltrating. However, he wanted to hear what others had to say. He knew that the mess tents were the place to gather scuttlebutt.

Toting his rifle, Cole headed toward the mess tent. His career in the kitchen itself hadn't lasted long, thank goodness, but that didn't stop him from stopping by for a sandwich and a hot cup of coffee. Even when regular chow wasn't being served, there was always something to eat and hot coffee if you knew who to ask.

"It's good to see you with that rifle," the mess sergeant said. "I never could figure you for a guy who toted a spatula."

"I reckon someone's got to keep the Chinese from coming over here and stealing all the pancakes. You ain't gonna fight them off with a spatula."

The sergeant snorted. "Don't be so sure about that. We aren't totally defenseless. You shoulda seen our last batch of biscuits. Those things could have doubled as grenades."

Cole grinned. "Thanks for the coffee. Keep that spatula handy."

Hanging around the mess tent, Cole started asking around and struck up a conversation with some guys from a squad that had rotated back from protecting the flank.

"Did you all hear about the Chinese sneaking in here last night?" he asked. "They tore the place up."

"Yeah, we heard all about it," said a soldier, sucking deeply on a cigarette. "I'll bet they came through our section. We can hear them for sure, but we can't see them. It's darker than Mao's asshole out there at night."

"Well, they can't see in the dark any better than we can," Cole pointed out. "How are they finding their way through our lines?"

"I can tell you one thing, buddy," the soldier said, warming to the conversation now that someone was interested in what he had to say. "We've passed this along, but nobody believes us. They think we're nuts."

"Ain't nothin' them Chinese do that would surprise me anymore," Cole said.

"You got that right. That's what I'm saying, you know? What happens is that sometimes in the morning we'll see a little white trail of powder on the ground. I don't know what it is. Maybe flour. Maybe lime. Maybe the ground-up bones of all the Chinese folks who didn't agree with the Communists."

Cole nodded. "Go on."

"It's real strange, but it seems to me that what's happening is that the Chinese have themselves a scout going through and leading the way, and once they found their way through, they are sending the rest of their squad along that trail. Anyhow, that's what I think."

Cole said, "Makes sense to me. Maybe somebody at headquarters needs to start listening to what you've got to say."

"I won't hold my breath," the soldier said. "Say, is there any more of that coffee around here?"

"Go on back to the kitchen and them 'em that the hillbilly sent you."

"The hillbilly. Hah, I like that." The soldier seemed to notice Cole's rifle for the first time. "You're that sniper I heard about? Shoot some for me. I tell you what, though. If you come through our section, tell the guys first so that they don't shoot you by accident. Some of the guys are getting trigger happy, if you know what I mean. These Chinese have 'em spooked."

The soldier and his buddies went in search of more hot coffee.

Cole had been right about how the Chinese were reaching the American lines. The method that they used to mark their trail was something new and useful. He supposed that he should be thankful that the Chinese had already done the hard part by finding a way between the ridges. Now it was his turn to turn the tables and get behind the Chinese lines to get the drop on that enemy sniper.

He would just have to hurry up and get the job done before the counter-attack on Sniper Ridge.

* * *

DARKNESS WAS FALLING by the time Cole returned to his tent. The other guys were sitting on the ground in the last of the light, smoking cigarettes, and starting to shiver as the autumn chill increased. Sometimes, quick fires were made, but no one sat around them for long due to the threat of Chinese snipers, who could easily have crept close enough to pick out targets in the firelight. One by one, the soldiers in the squad peeled off for their tents and the warmth of their sleeping bags.

But not Cole. He was just getting started.

He spread a blanket in front of his tent and lit a candle. He then set his rifle on the blanket, with his intention being to give it a good cleaning. The feeble, flickering light was just enough for him to work by without drawing any unwanted attention from the enemy. There was also something timeless about the flame. It could just have easily have been one of his ancestors, cleaning a Kentucky long rifle by firelight.

Sitting Indian-style on the ground, he set to work. There was already a running joke that Cole had the cleanest rifle in Korea.

Pomeroy used to kid him, "Hillbilly, you could do surgery with that rifle."

"What kind of operation would I do with a rifle?"

"You could remove someone's appendix, or shoot out their heart—"

"Surgery," Cole said.

He took the rifle apart now, laying the pieces out on the blanket. He took off the scope, shucked out the bolt, and disassembled the trigger mechanism. He then began cleaning the rifle, working through the bore with the patch and gun solvent, swirling out the powder residue and even tiny unseen bits from the bullet jacket.

Any bit of grit wedged in the rifling could potentially throw off the accuracy of the bullet, so his goal was to make the barrel as clean as when it had left the hands of the machinist. When he was done, that barrel and that rifle would be a slick as a whistle.

He worked several white cotton patches through the bore until they came out clean. When he held the barrel up and looked through it into the candle flame, the rifling reflecting the light in all of its well-oiled, precision-machined glory.

If he could have crawled through that barrel toward that light, he was sure that he could have found God on the other side.

Next, he went to work on the chamber, the bolt, and the trigger assembly. He used a fine brush to scrub them clean of any powder or metal residue, then rubbed them down with gun oil. His fingers began to grow a little numb in the cool air, but Cole was so engrossed in his work that he didn't notice. He worked until the smooth steel felt buttery under his fingertips.

Back home, he had started making custom hunting knives, taking up the trade that his old friend Hollis had practiced in his mountaintop forge. It had been Hollis who made Cole's Bowie knife with its razor-sharp, Damascus steel blade. A soldier now had that knife, having stolen it off Cole. The thought rankled him.

When Hollis had passed, before Cole returned from the last war in

Europe, he had left all his tools, even his shop, to Cole. It had been the best thing that anyone had ever done for him. Hollis must have known that someone like Cole would lose himself in the craft. It had certainly kept him away from the darker corners of his mind—and from the whiskey bottle that had been his own Pa's downfall.

Cole had found that he was good at the precision work required for making knives, though not yet as good as Hollis had been. If he ever got home again, he would be glad to get back to turning blanks of steel into knives, improving his craft with each one.

When Cole was finished with the rifle, he looked at all the pieces spread out on the blanket. By themselves, they were simply parts. Chunks of metal. One by one, he reassembled them expertly, each piece of metal fitting smoothly into the other until the rifle was whole again, gleaming and deadly with purpose.

Cole took the rifle back to the tent where, once again, the kid was already asleep, exhausted from a day of sentry duty. Cole felt tired himself, and he felt that pang of hunger in his belly, a good kind of hunger, an ache of animal drive.

He reckoned that maybe he'd just had a run of bad luck up there across from Sniper Ridge, but he was going to show the Chinese enemy that on a good day, there was no beating Caje Cole.

He curled himself around the rifle and slept a blessedly dreamless sleep.

CHAPTER TWENTY-TWO

COLE WAS up before first light, the critter deep within him uncurling its claws as he set out from camp in a killing mood. The morning dawned cold and crisp, sharp as the edge of a knife and gleaming like a blade once the sun crept over the mountaintops. The rifle felt cold and deadly in his hands.

His preparations the previous day had honed him to a sharp point, but the truth was, he had been preparing for moments like this his whole life. He was a hunter by nature. Now, it was time to hunt the enemy.

His time might be limited. The orders that had come around for another attack on Sniper Ridge meant that he might be on the wrong side when the shooting started. He would just have to figure that out when the time came.

Leaving alone felt right because this was a one-man job. He didn't need to worry about getting anyone else killed. It was going to come down to him and the Chinese sniper. One of them was not going to survive this morning, and Cole was determined to make sure that it was going to be the other guy who didn't make it.

His plan was a little crazy, the kind of thing you usually cooked up over too much moonshine and then worked to forget about the next morning, along with your aching head. But Cole set out to make it happen. As he climbed the ridge he thought, ain't no goin' back *now*.

He climbed toward the front line of American defenses, off on the left flank. The men were more spread out here because the threat of a full-on Chinese attack was unlikely. The heaviest defenses were centered along the lower point of the ridge above the base camp. The Americans depended on the rough landscape itself to do a better job of defending their position than any rows of concertina wire.

He spoke in a hushed tone to a couple of soldiers in a foxhole.

"Been quiet around here?"

"Thought we heard some enemy troops last night, but didn't see anything," the GI said.

Cole nodded. "You probably heard right. My guess is that they come and go through here. Listen, I'm gonna move out in front of you. Spread the word. Don't go shooting me."

"You're headed the wrong way," the GI told him. "Nothing out there but rocks and Chinese."

"That's the idea," Cole said.

The GI looked from Cole to the scoped rifle in his hands. "You're a sniper, huh? What are you gonna do, sneak closer and pick off some of the enemy?"

"Well, I sure as hell ain't gonna cook 'em breakfast," Cole said. "Now, keep your fool heads down if any shooting starts. Just so you know, if I come back, I'll likely be hauling ass."

"If you come back?"

"Like I said, if I come back."

Leaving the GIs something to think about, he slipped through the line of defenses and began walking parallel to it. The soldiers back in the foxhole had said that they might have heard enemy troops moving around in the dark. Their ears had not been playing tricks on them.

It was no secret that groups of Chinese saboteurs constantly slipped through the lines to do whatever damage they could. The raids were yet another way that they wore down their enemy. Interestingly enough, the UN and American forces didn't go much for that approach. Part of it was simple fear. If the Chinese raiders were captured, which did sometimes happen, they became prisoners of war.

Nobody much liked the chances for any American raiders captured by the Chinese. The best they could hope for was torture and death.

Something that had been learned from the captured troops was how they picked their way through the American lines. Cole had heard rumors about it, and he thought that he could put that knowledge to use.

For too long, the enemy had been bringing the war to the Americans. Now, he was going to bring the war to them.

Not far from the foxhole where he had encountered the GIs, Cole found what he was looking for. *I'll be damned.* The rumors were true. Those raiders hadn't been lying about how they got through the US lines.

Cole looked more closely. It was a sign so faint that most eyes would have missed it. But Cole was a natural tracker, having grown up hunting in the mountains. His eyes could pick out a broken twig or the faintest impression of a footprint on a mountain trail. The markings that he saw now leaped out at him like a road sign.

Coming down through the hills was the faintest line of white powder. It wasn't at all like the sideline on a football field, but more like the spillage from an hourglass. In some places, the line was thicker and in other places it disappeared for a few paces, only to reappear in spurts like dots and dashes on the ground. If you didn't know it was there and you weren't looking for it, your eyes would have dismissed it.

Here and there, the line went up over some rocks or around a boulder. Tellingly, the trail tended to follow any natural cover that helped screen the path from the American sentries ahead.

Cole wet a finger, then bent down and tasted the powder. Bland, but he detected the faint taste of flour. It was the perfect marker because it lasted just long enough before fading into the rocky soil.

He had to give it to the Chinese. He could picture just how they were doing it. They were sending a lone scout to find his way through the American defenses. If they lost one man, so be it. One man could have moved silently through the defenses.

He likely probed the line until he found a way through, a spot where the trenches or foxholes were just a little too far apart or where a rocky outcropping broke up the line of sight, enabling someone to slip through unseen. Cole shook his head in wonder. Sneaky bastards.

Cole couldn't help but think of a finger poked through a hole in a sweater, or maybe a hernia jutting through an abdominal wall. The enemy was looking for a weakness. Once the enemy scout had found that soft spot, he retraced his steps, this time with a bag of flour that leaked a thin stream down onto the ground, marking his path. Later that night or the next night, a raiding party could follow the trail, slipping unseen through the American lines. It was a regular saboteur's highway.

One thing about the Chinese, Cole thought, was that they were good at being sneaky. It was how they were going to win this war—that and their willingness to throw away their own lives like you threw handfuls of corn to greedy hens.

But the Chinese saboteurs were not the only ones who could move silently through the landscape. Cole did that now, retracing the path that went deep into the rocky ravines surrounding the American position. He passed through thickets and clambered over rocks, moving silently as the sun climbing the morning sky.

You could almost say this was Indian country in that neither side bothered defending it because it was too rough. Behind him was the American line. Somewhere up ahead was the Chinese line.

Easy now. The critter part of him was intent on killing, driven by it, like a wolf with an empty belly. But the cold part of Cole's mind reminded him that the hunter needed to be silent. One misstep, one snapped twig, one clatter of rocks under his boots—and he would surely unleash a hail of enemy machine gun fire. Wouldn't that just cancel Christmas?

Now came the tricky part. It was his turn to get through the Chinese lines. He had to beat them at their own game.

Moving forward, he could actually smell the Chinese before he heard them. It wasn't any kind of judgment about the Chinese themselves, but only the fact that they smelled different, like garlic and stale rice and maybe some seaweed mixed in. Germans had their own smell back in the last war. Like beer and sausage. The Japs had their own smell, too, from what he'd heard. The enemy claimed that the Americans smelled like old hamburgers.

This idea of defining smells might have seemed like foolishness to some, but he knew that in the woods, you could smell game, too—the musky scent of where a fox or coyote marked its territory, or the almost sweet smell the deer left behind where they had bedded down, not all that different from the barn smell of cattle. In part, Cole had given up cigarettes for good in an effort to detect these smells.

Creeping closer, he now heard voices. Speaking in that peculiar sing-song language. It was funny—as much as they'd been fighting the Chinese, they rarely ever heard them talk—except when they were screaming during a bayonet assault. That didn't need any translation.

Cole couldn't understand the words, of course, but he found the rhythm of the language soothing. It wasn't at all harsh and guttural like German—or English, for that matter.

The fact that the Chinese were talking among themselves, even laughing quietly, was a good sign. They wouldn't be listening too hard for trouble, and they certainly weren't expecting him. This white line marked a one-way street, anyhow, as far as the Chinese were concerned.

Coming back the other way wasn't gonna be as easy, if you could call this easy. If he came back at all, as he had said to the sentry, he was gonna be damn lucky.

Now came the hard part. He actually had to slip between the Chinese foxholes and get behind their line. Darkness would have helped, and he had thought about doing this at night, but had ruled that out. First of all, he wouldn't have been able to see a damn thing. He might have crawled right into an enemy foxhole. Second, the sentries would be on alert at night. Finally, it might have been his bad luck to run smack dab into one of those raiding squads. Instead, he had opted to wait for daylight and depend on his stealthiest skills.

Out here on the flank, nobody had bothered to cut down the brush between foxholes, which worked to Cole's advantage. He slung the rifle over his shoulder so that it hung crosswise across his back, then got down on his belly. Quietly, he slithered in under the bushes.

He had encountered more than a few snakes in these hills—the

Asian pit vipers that were like a deadlier version of a copperhead particularly liked the rocky landscape—but he hoped it was cold enough now to have sent them into their winter dens. Besides, if the enemy heard him, snakes were going to be the least of his worries.

Cole crept forward, pushing his way through the thickest branches and dry, saw-edged grasses that cut at his face. The enemy's voices were so close now that he had to force himself to remember to breathe. Maybe he had steered too close to a foxhole, but he had no choice but to keep going. *Can't stop now.* No way could he get himself turned around without being heard. The only way out of this mess was straight ahead, so he kept crawling.

Something moved in the brush off to his right and Cole froze. Automatically, his hand went to his knife. It was a standard-issue combat knife, not the hand-forged Bowie knife that he had lost at the Chosin when he was briefly captured, but Cole had honed this blade to a wickedly sharp edge. Slowly, he eased the knife out of the sheath.

The movement stopped. He heard a satisfied grunt, and then came the unmistakable sound of a stream of urine pattering on the ground. So damn close it almost splashed him. Cole froze. The Chinese soldier farted loudly, sighed contentedly, then buttoned up and moved away. He was sure that the Chinese had designated latrine areas, but out here, if there were no officers around, who cared? It was easier to take a few steps away to relieve yourself. That soldier couldn't have known how close he'd come to getting stabbed.

Cole moved on, right through a damp place that was likely courtesy of the soldier, but all he cared about was being silent. Slowly, each move calculated, he moved forward until the sounds from the foxhole faded a bit and moved around to his rear quadrant. He had managed to sneak right past the enemy.

The brush began to thin, giving way to a boulder-strewn field, like the backwash from some long-ago flood. Keeping low, he worked his way through the boulders, thankful that the ground was too rough for the Chinese to have dug any foxholes here. He was now on Sniper Ridge, to the east of the center where the bulk of the two armies faced each other. Nobody seemed to be around, and there wasn't any sign of established enemy occupation in this section. No roads, no telephone lines. Just rocks and brush. Just the way he liked it.

Cole moved east toward the center of the line, following the northern face of the ridge, behind where the enemy line was located. His plan was to stealthily move parallel to the enemy position, keeping out of sight using whatever cover was available, until he came to the center where the enemy sniper had been hidden on the previous days. With any luck, Cole would be right behind him.

But first, Cole had to get there. If sneaking through the enemy position was a crazy idea, there weren't even any words to describe what he was doing now. Bat shit crazy? That came close.

Of course, he was breaking every goddamn rule he could think of. If the Chinese caught him, they'd likely shoot him as a spy. Maybe torture him first. As for his own side, he hadn't asked for permission to go on this one-man mission because he was sure nobody would have given it. What if he never came back? He grinned. Desertion wasn't much of an issue in Korea. Where the hell would anyone go? Wasn't anything or anyone that was real welcoming in this place. Nope—Lieutenant Ballard and all the rest would just figure that Cole had fallen off a cliff somewhere.

Not that Cole gave a damn. He had some business to settle.

Pushing all other thoughts out of his mind, he kept moving, keeping to the brush and boulders. Once or twice he crossed a path leading down from the face of the ridge, but didn't encounter anyone moving up or down to the Chinese line.

Eventually, he reached a path that was bigger and wider than the rest—big enough for numbers of men or maybe even artillery to be dragged into position. He must be near the Chinese center. Off in the distance, he saw a few tents, even a wisp or two of smoke rising into the still morning air. With a shock, he realized that he could actually see the Chinese HQ. *Holy hell, Hillbilly, this shit is gettin' real.*

He turned south now and began bushwhacking toward the peak of the ridge itself. The ridge ran like the back of a bony, swaybacked mule, narrow in some of the high places, lower and wider in others. He got onto one of these high places so that when he raised his head above the rocks and brush, he could see down the length of the mule's spine.

From here, he could see the network of Chinese defenses: men in their trenches and foxholes, machine gun nests, a bunker or two that must have sheltered command centers. It was like a goddamn army of ants. Chinese ants.

Almost directly beneath him was a knobby outcropping that he had memorized all too well from staring at it from the opposite direction. The landmark was known as Mao's Ears. The enemy sniper was somewhere down there.

Moving his scope slowly, slowly over the surrounding foxholes and trenches, he searched every square foot. He could see what was invisible from the American side. From here, he could see the back end of the Chinese position.

Finally, he spotted what he was looking for. A Chinese soldier, crouched in a hole, peering through a rifle with a telescopic sight. To his surprise, it was only the sniper by himself this morning. What had become of the spotter? Never mind; it just made Cole's job a fraction easier. One man to eliminate, instead of two.

In spite of himself, Cole felt his heart quicken. His sights were already on the sniper's back. Wasn't even that hard of a shot. Hell, at this range, he could have taken out his pistol and had a good chance of hitting him. All that he had to do was squeeze the trigger.

But not yet. The absence of the enemy sniper's spotter reminded Cole that he had better pay attention to his own surroundings. Cole was on his own here—he wasn't getting any help. Without anyone to watch his back, it was possible for someone to sneak right up on him. His plan would go all to pieces if he got back shot right about now. Hell now, that would ruin his whole day.

He turned away from the ridge and swept his scope across the landscape around him. He didn't see anything threatening.

Behind him, looking down, he also had a good view of the distant Chinese HQ. Out of curiosity, he put the scope to his eye and saw the movement of troops and vehicles. It was a long ways off, but in the still air, he felt confident that he could have sent a bullet down there if the need arose. He watched for a while through the scope. There seemed to be some commotion as more vehicles arrived and some of the Chinese brass got out. A knot of what must be officers surrounded one man in particular, apparently out of deference.

There wasn't anything special about the man that Cole could see, other than the fact that his frame looked somewhat older and heavier. The Chinese didn't go much for fancy uniforms. However, he was clearly a man of some importance. He turned to say something to an aide, who went racing away on some errand. *That there has got to be a Chinese general.*

Cole thought about that. He hadn't come all this way to shoot a general. Hadn't been his plan at all. But here was the opportunity, staring at him right through the rifle scope. It was like he'd gone squirrel huntin' and walked right up on a big ol' twelve-point buck. A man would be a fool to stick with the plan and shoot at squirrels instead.

Cole felt torn. He owed it to Pomeroy to shoot this sniper. He owed it to all those dead and wounded American boys he had seen in the field hospital. This sniper had done that to them. He had come all this way to triumph over his enemy, even had him in his sights, and yet, the general could be the more important target.

He paused, thinking it over. If he fired first at the general, the enemy sniper was so close that he would hear the shot and be alerted. Cole might lose his chance.

Already, he was running out of time. In the distance, he heard the concussive *whump* of artillery firing. Rounds began to strike the ridge far to his right, sending the enemy scurrying. The beginning of the artillery barrage could only mean that the planned attack had begun. The artillery fire walked back from the ridge, even with where Cole was hiding, although not in the area he was in. He had to hurry it up before all hell broke loose or the artillery shifted its aim and pulverized him in the process.

Taking his eye off the scope, he looked at the sniper, still in his hole, then down at the Chinese HQ that was a lot farther down the ridge.

He had to decide, right now. Shoot that general, or the sniper?

CHAPTER TWENTY-THREE

His mind made up, Cole swung the rifle toward the headquarters compound. He had come out here to square things up with the sniper, but wouldn't it be better to strike fear right into the hearts of the enemy?

He might very well be losing his chance at the sniper, but it was a chance that he would have to take. He had two targets here, and he had chosen which one to shoot at first.

Unbidden, words of advice came to mind right from his old friend Vaccaro, from back in the last war. *When you find yourself in bed with two women, screw the ugly one first.* It was a crude sentiment, but Cole smirked at the memory. It was highly unlikely that Vaccaro had been presented with that dilemma, much as he likely dreamed about it. But that nugget of wisdom applied to more than one situation.

Cole was going to shoot the ugly one first.

The headquarters shot was the hardest one to make. Unfortunately, Cole was close enough that the other sniper would surely hear the crack of his rifle. Any hope of surprising the enemy sniper would be gone. And with the element of surprise gone, so would be Cole's chances of slipping back to his own lines without a fight. Plus, it looked as if he would be running right into the arms of a full-fledged attack.

Pushing those thoughts from his mind, he settled his sights on the distant throng of VIPs, picking out the man who stood apart from the others. Through the scope, Cole could see that the man was bare-headed, while the others all wore officer's caps of some kind. It was too far away to make out any of the man's features. Some part of him knew that he had better hurry because the man, whoever he was, wasn't going to stand there forever. The opportunity would be lost.

Then again, some things could not be hurried.

It was a long way to shoot a rifle. Feeling the challenge of it, his senses quickened and wrestled with one another, making him feel both restless and calm. He chose to focus on being calm. His breathing slowed, then stopped. Even Cole's heartbeat seemed to check itself.

He felt the slightest of breezes against his cheek. His practiced eye raised the crosshairs to the quadrant just above and to the right of the target.

The morning sun was higher now, and he worried about the glint from the glass lens of his telescope. A sniper couldn't control every-thing. Then again, nobody down there would be looking for him or expecting him, which made what he was about to do all the more devastating.

Ideally, he planned to time his shot just as one of the artillery shells exploded, thus masking the crack of his rifle. That shouldn't be all that hard, considering that the shells were falling hard and fast now.

Ever so slowly, his finger took up the tension on the trigger. He became aware of just two things in all this world—what his eye saw through the scope, and the silken metal beneath his fingertip.

A shell whistled, struck the ridge off to his left, and Cole fired.

Fast as a bullet moved, outpacing sound itself, its brass-jacketed spearpoint still required time to cover the distance to the target.

Cole still held his breath.

One Mississippi, two—

Through the scope, he saw the target crumple. He breathed again.

Down in the enemy headquarters, there was pandemonium. Staff officers ducked their heads, looking in every direction, for at this distance it was impossible to tell the origin of the bullet. There had been just the one shot. It was all that Cole needed.

Whom had he killed? To Cole, it didn't matter. He had struck at the enemy and taken some measure of revenge for all those American boys lost in the march from the Chosin or cut down in the fight for these godforsaken hilltops. For Cole, the morning sun seemed to shine a little brighter.

But his business here was far from over. He swung around until he was facing the Chinese line. Already, the artillery bombardment was slackening, but the small arms fire had increased in the distance. All along the Chinese line, rifles and machine guns fired mercilessly, which could only mean one thing—the counterattack against Sniper Ridge had begun. Cole's fellow Americans planned on taking back the ridge that they had already won, and then lost again.

He would join that fight if he could, but for now, there was only one enemy soldier that he was concerned about.

Cole didn't need the scope to see the sniper. The son of a bitch must have heard the shot from behind him and had turned around. Like Cole, he was using his eyes rather than the magnified but narrow field of view provided by the rifle scope. The enemy sniper was looking this way and that, which told Cole that he hadn't been spotted yet.

Cole was still down in the rocks, hidden from sight. He had the advantage in that while the enemy sniper suspected something wasn't right, he didn't know where to look. Cole, on the other hand, knew exactly where his target was located.

Quickly, Cole found him through the scope. He was close enough to see the enemy's face. With a shock, Cole realized this was the same Chinese sniper who had captured him at the Chosin Reservoir. He would have recognized that ugly bastard anywhere.

Cole and the other soldiers captured with him—with the exception of one who had been outright murdered by the Chinese—had managed to escape. The enemy sniper hadn't been willing to let them go and had tracked them and harassed them right across the frozen ice of the reservoir itself. Cole had left a trap for the pursuers, but it appeared that this soldier had escaped.

Quickly, Cole found him through the scope. He settled the

crosshairs on him. All that Cole had to do now was squeeze the trigger. His finger pressed on the smooth metal—and stopped.

Something about this was far too easy. Cole wanted this bastard to see who was punching his ticket.

Keeping the rifle to his shoulder, with the sight never wavering from the enemy, Cole slowly rose from cover. The enemy sniper still didn't have his rifle to his own shoulder, which was a mistake on his part. Now, he saw Cole rising up. Through the scope, Cole could see the other man's look of astonishment. They might not speak the same language, but that look needed no translation.

The other sniper knew that Cole had him dead to rights, but that didn't stop him from springing into action, trying to get his own weapon into play.

Cole was ready for him. His trigger finger tensed ever so slightly, releasing the firing pin into the center of the brass-jacketed cartridge in the chamber. Instantly, the bullet left the rifle. The enemy soldier toppled as he was struck with more than two thousand foot-pounds of good ol' American whomp ass.

Cole worked the bolt, then climbed out of his rocky hiding place. He moved toward the enemy sniper nest as if moving through a tunnel, oblivious of the battle beginning to unfold around him.

He reached the trench and jumped in, then stared down at the body. With professional interest, he noted that the bullet had ripped through the other man's heart. A killing shot if ever there was one. He would have been aware for a moment or two of what was happening, and then the final oblivion.

The other sniper was a small man, his body looking even smaller in death. His uniform looked well-used, much like Cole's, in point of fact. Finally, Cole reached down and removed the big Bowie knife that the enemy sniper still wore. This had been taken from Cole months ago when he was captured. It had been made by his old friend Hollis Bailey's own hands, and Cole was glad to have it back.

"About time I got my knife back, you thievin' son of a bitch," he muttered.

Cole felt a wave of anger. There wasn't anything else that he could do to the sniper, who was now beyond the reach of his revenge. But Cole wasn't done yet.

Cole picked up the rifle. It was Russian, a Mosin-Nagant being more than a little familiar to Cole, it being one of the superior sniper weapons of the last war and just as deadly in this one. Although it was hardly an elegant rifle, it was sturdy and efficient. This one looked battered and well-used, its stock scarred and the finish worn away from being held against a cheek, locked into the shooter.

Cole set down his own Springfield and picked up the Russian rifle. With practiced hands, he shucked out the bolt and threw it far out into the muddy surroundings, where it would never be found. He unfastened the scope and then smashed it under his boot.

He lacked any tools to destroy the rifle itself, so he did the next best thing. He wedged the barrel between two big rocks—no shortage of those around here—and tried to lever those boulders out of place, grunting and straining with the effort. After a minute, working until his muscles burned, he was sure that the rifle would never shoot straight again.

That was some satisfaction, at least. He also felt calmer now.

Gathering himself, he realized with some surprise that he had tuned out the chatter of gunfire all around him. He had been too busy eliminating some sort of Chinese Grand Poobah, as well as the enemy sniper, to pay a whole lot of attention to what was unfolding around him.

The shooting that he had done was just the beginning of more to come. From the sounds of it, Cole now had a whole new battle to fight.

With a growing sense of dread, he realized that he was on the wrong side of a few thousand Chinese troops, and he would have to find a way through if he ever hoped to get back to the American lines again.

CHAPTER TWENTY-FOUR

COLE DIDN'T HAVE a lot of options, except to get the hell out of there. All hell was breaking loose with this American attack on the ridge. On the one hand, the attack had been a good distraction, drawing the attention of the Chinese defenders, but he hadn't counted on getting caught up on the wrong side of it.

There were foxholes filled with enemy soldiers on his right and left. It was only a matter of time before somebody came along and noticed that he didn't belong there. Things would get a little hot then.

He took a quick peek over the edge of the dead sniper's trench. He could hear firing all around him, but caught only glimpses of the padded Chinese uniforms or their *Ushanka*-style caps. If they happened to look up and notice him, he'd be a goner. Time to get out of Dodge.

He scrambled up out of the trench and started running back the way he had come, roughly following his original path. He made sure to zigzag as he ran, just in case one of the enemy spotted him. He didn't want to be an easy target.

He came to the wide path that he had crossed coming up the back-side of the ridge. He had been lucky that first time around and hadn't seen anyone, but his luck had just run out.

He ran smack dab into the path of a Chinese platoon, moving on the double to reinforce the soldiers under attack. Cole burst out of the underbrush just ahead of them, appearing so suddenly that the lead soldiers halted in surprise. The troops still coming up the trail behind them piled up behind them like water behind a dam.

For the longest of seconds, he and the Chinese stood there, blinking at each other in astonishment.

However, the element of surprise did not last long.

One of the soldiers actually shouted in outrage—or maybe in terror.

I know just how you feel, buddy.

An officer, or maybe a sergeant, started shouting commands. As fast as you could say lickety-split, several rifles were pointed at Cole.

He responded by raising his rifle and firing it point-blank at the nearest soldier. The startled Chinese troops fired back, but Cole was already tearing through the scrub trees on the other side of the path. Bullets zipped around him, but the entire platoon didn't give chase. That would have been quite a rabbit hunt, with Cole as the rabbit. Instead, a couple of soldiers peeled off to go after Cole, while the rest of the unit moved on toward the front line, where there were a whole lot more American soldiers to worry about.

Behind him, he could hear the soldiers crashing through the brush in pursuit, firing as they ran. Cole dropped to one knee and waited until he had a clear shot. He pulled the trigger. One down.

The second man threw himself flat and blasted away in Cole's direction with what sounded like a captured burp gun. Bullets flickered overhead, turning the branches into toothpicks. Cole kept himself as low to the ground as possible.

When the enemy soldier took his finger off the trigger—or perhaps he had run out of ammo—Cole fired at where he had last seen the muzzle flash. He rolled to his feet and kept running. He didn't hear anyone behind him. Either he'd gotten lucky with the shot, or his pursuer had decided that chasing him off was good enough.

In any case, one pursuing soldier was the least of his worries. The artillery was really chewing up the ridge, throwing geysers of dirt and rock around. Chunks of red-hot shrapnel sounded like a whickering horse as it cut the air. He ran down the slope, away from the ridge, to avoid the bursting shells, but a few still overshot the target and exploded in the rear.

Breathing heavily, he finally reached the section of the Chinese line where he had sneaked through earlier. He knew that getting past the enemy troops this time around would be even harder because they would be on high alert.

What he hadn't counted on was there being a lot more troops. This had been the sleepy end of the flank, but it wasn't anymore.

Crouched in the shrubs, he caught his breath and stared in amazement at the swarm of enemy soldiers who now filled the area. Before, there had been just a handful.

Briefly, he worried that they were there to catch him. Maybe word had gotten out that there was a sniper behind their lines. *Good lord, I hope they ain't waitin' for me.*

However, the troops here seemed to be preparing for the attack. All at once, Cole understood what was happening. While the American attack was happening at the center of the line, the Chinese were planning a counter-attack on the American flank. Worse, they might slip around the flank altogether and attack the rear, targeting the camp itself.

If that happened, the American attack might fall to pieces as men were called back to defend HQ or worse yet, found themselves surrounded.

This was a classic Chinese tactic. Swarm the line and hope to break through. Attack the flanks and slip into the rear. Cole had to admit, the enemy was the master of the surprise attack. And he had just stumbled right into the middle of it.

Maybe he could throw a wrench into the works.

Cole took stock. He had the Springfield and plenty of ammunition. There was a Browning 1911 .45 strapped to his hip. He carried two hand grenades. And if worse came to worse, he even had his old Bowie knife back. He pulled the blade from the sheath and inspected it. He saw with satisfaction that the blade still gleamed. At least the Chinese sniper knew enough to take good care of a knife.

Time to get to work if he was going to stop—or at least, slow down —this Chinese sneak attack on the American flank.

Just me and about fifty Chinese fellers, Cole thought. *Pretty good odds.*

But first, he needed a better place from which to shoot. Although he had concealment, he was too exposed to return fire. He needed to find some cover.

Keeping low, he skirted the enemy position and moved toward a knoll that rose just behind it. There were a couple of big rocks up there that would do nicely for what he had in mind.

The troops seemed to be organizing themselves, getting ready to move out, so Cole moved faster. The knoll gave him a vantage point of maybe six feet. He wedged himself down between two big rocks, leaving him a kind of rocky V that he could shoot through while being able to see the bulk of the troops nearby. The range wasn't more than a couple of hundred feet. Easy pickings. The problem was that the enemy wouldn't have any trouble figuring out where the shooting was coming from. Once that happened, things would get mighty hot for him up on this knoll.

Cole picked out what looked like an officer, lined up the crosshairs, and fired. No sooner had the man gone down, then he had another round in the chamber. He picked another target, fired. And again.

Below, the enemy scattered, some going to ground in the few foxholes or just diving into the brush. Whenever somebody got the fool notion to show his head, Cole took it off.

It didn't take long for the enemy to figure out that they were under attack by just one sniper—or where that sniper was hidden. Just as Cole had predicted, bullets began to ricochet off the boulders. Lucky for him, they didn't seem to have a machine gun. But if they brought up a mortar, it would all be over.

A bullet struck the rock near his face, a fragment of rock or lead stinging his cheek. More bullets came in as the Chinese directed fire at him, forcing him to keep his head down rather than shoot back.

Can't stay here. If he did, either a lucky shot would find him or the Chinese would flank him—carrying out a miniature version of the maneuver they were planning for the attacking American force.

Cole got an idea. He took off his helmet and wedged it into the rocky V. Now, the enemy had a target. The Chinese obliged him by increasing their rate of fire.

He didn't plan to stick around. Instead, Cole slipped out from behind the rocks, keeping low, and moved off the knoll and back into the underbrush. He popped up long enough to take a shot at one of the enemy soldiers, then dropped back down. He was hidden for now, but once they figured out that he wasn't on the knoll anymore, they would start chewing up the brush—and Cole along with it. The only solution was to keep moving and stay ahead of them.

He popped up and fired, dropping another one of the enemy. Then he kept moving.

Up ahead, the brush started to thin out and the landscape opened up into barren, rocky scree. He didn't like his chances trying to cross that, but there was more brush on the other side where he could lose himself.

He popped up and fired again. The enemy was figuring this out, though. Bullets began to pepper the long grass and chew through the woody shrubs.

Cole braced himself for the dash across the scree. He didn't like his chances, but if he could just get across it—

There was a shout from the enemy, and the fire began to slacken as it was redirected in the opposite direction.

He soon saw why. An American unit was advancing toward the Chinese, emerging from the brush of no-man's land between the two lines. Cole grinned. Apparently, the Chinese weren't the only ones who had caught on to the idea of sneak attacks. This unit was trying to flank the Chinese position and maybe come around behind them.

Faced with this new threat, the enemy troops forget all about Cole.

He ran back to the knoll, grabbed his helmet, and got back on the rifle. One by one, the enemy defenders either dropped or fled.

Once the American troops approached, Cole took off his helmet again and waved it at them so that they would know he wasn't Chinese.

A sergeant approached, staring at Cole's scoped sniper rifle in amazement. "You just wiped out half of that unit, soldier. I wondered who was back here, helping us out. Where the hell did you come from?"

"Me? Why, I reckon I'm from Tennessee," he drawled.

The sergeant shook his head. "Crazy goddamn hillbilly," he muttered.

CHAPTER TWENTY-FIVE

IN THE VALLEY below the ridge, Lieutenant Ballard was leading his platoon through a hail of gunfire. The attack was on to recapture Sniper Ridge.

Turning to assess how his men were positioned, he watched with dismay as his radioman was hit in the chest, the round passing all the way through Private Gordy and bursting out through the radio itself. Gordy toppled forward under the weight of the radio and didn't move again.

Cursing, Ballard reached down to grab Gordy by the shoulder, turning him just enough to see the sightless eyes. The poor son of a bitch was already dead—as was the radio.

The lieutenant carried one of the new-fangled M-2 carbines, a short-barreled affair that Ballard had pulled some rank to obtain because he liked the idea of carrying the newest and best. Also, the carbine could be fired on a fully automatic setting, although that chewed right through the 30-found magazine.

Ballard was a tall man, and the weapon looked extra small in his big, gangly hands. To be sure, he was regretting the choice right now because the carbine resembled a child's pop gun rather than a serious weapon.

Leveling the carbine at the top of the ridge, he fired several shots at the Chinese defenders. *Take that, you sons of bitches.* He was sure that he hadn't hit a thing, but it made him feel better.

The apex of the steep ridge was the objective of their attack. Once again, it didn't help that all the enemy troops up there had to do to defend the ridge was to throw rocks down on the attackers. That was something of an exaggeration, but it wasn't far from the truth.

Ballard thought that it didn't help that they had already made this attack a few days before, across this same rough terrain. Although they had managed to capture the ridge, the company that had been left to hold the ridge had been overwhelmed by a nighttime Chinese counter-attack. Now, they were trying to get it back again.

With the radio out of commission, Ballard was going to need a runner to carry messages. Preferably someone small and quick, who wouldn't be missed much in the actual attack.

Looking around again, he caught sight of the kid with glasses. Tommy Wilson. He seemed to recall something about Wilson having played football back in high school. Plus, he was within earshot.

"Wilson! Get over here!" The kid scrambled to the lieutenant's side, both of them taking a knee as bullets whined overhead. Lucky for them, the tendency was to overshoot when firing downhill, which the Chinese were doing now.

"Sir."

"I need you to take a message to Corporal Laurel. You know him?"

"Yes, sir."

"Tell him to move his squad right when we reach that gulch up there. He needs to make contact with the next platoon. We don't need any gaps."

"OK, sir."

"Now repeat that back to me."

Ballard had learned the hard way that half the time, messengers never remembered a damned thing in the heat of combat. He nodded with satisfaction when the kid repeated what he'd said verbatim. Maybe those glasses were proof that the kid wasn't a complete idiot.

The kid started to get up to deliver the message, but the Chinese fire up on the ridge intensified and Ballard pulled him back down. He looked up at the ridge and saw, incredulously, that a Chinese soldier stood up there on a rock, emptying a machine gun at Ballard's troops down below. Several men returned fire, but the man jumped back down, apparently unscathed.

What they needed was a sniper. Where the hell was that hillbilly when you needed him? Cole hadn't been present this morning when the platoon had formed up for the attack, a fact that rankled Ballard, although his absence wasn't all that unusual. Cole liked to be out before dawn, sniping at the Chinese.

Ballard thought again about how Cole had taken this bespectacled kid under his wing. Cole was a tough nut, but he seemed to have a soft spot for the kid. He'd also been loyal as hell to Pomeroy.

"Where the hell is Cole?" Ballard asked.

"He said he was going hunting this morning, sir."

The explanation had not immediately registered with Ballard. "Hunting for what?"

"Why, for Chinese, sir. What else?"

Hunting was one hell of a way to put it.

Now that the enemy fire had slackened, Ballard gave the kid a shove. "Go!"

Watching him run off, Ballard was thinking that they were going to need a miracle to pull off the attack this morning.

He got to his feet, waved the inadequate little carbine, and shouted, "Let's go, boys! We've got a hill to take!"

* * *

BALLARD LED his men forward up the hill, toward the peak of Sniper Ridge. Quickly, he checked the position of his platoon, knowing that the attack had to be coordinated. The idea was for the company to move in a straight line up the slope, putting constant pressure on the Chinese defenders.

"I want suppressing fire on that ridge," he shouted at the top of his lungs, straining to be heard over the din of weapons and incoming Chinese mortars.

"Yes, sir!" shouted back a couple of the men, their heads low over their rifles as they squeezed off round after round. The only way that they were going to push the Chinese off that hill was by sheer firepower.

Not that the Chinese were ready to give up. He could see their heads and shoulders up there, just as intent on shooting Americans as the Americans were on shooting the Chinese. Their deadly light machine guns chattered away at them, kicking up dirt and rocks as the gunners walked their fire toward the attackers.

Ballard ducked involuntarily as more shrapnel went flying by, the chunks so big that he could see them whir past like supersonic sparrows. Some claimed that they had found spent pieces stamped with names straight out of American factories—Kenmore, Ford, Fisher—indicating that the metal used to make Chinese ordnance had been sold to them from American scrapyards. Ballard didn't know if that was true, but he appreciated that there was a certain irony of getting cut in half by metal your own side had made.

Off to his right, he saw that his men were just where they should be. Ballard had started out in the center of his unit, but had now placed himself to the far left of his men so that he could more easily anchor them; he was the pin and they were the string on the map table.

Sergeant Weber came running over, crouched low, stopping once to help a man whose weapon had jammed. To say that Weber was cool under fire would have been an understatement.

"Sir, we need to pivot and hit them right at that gap."

"What gap?"

Weber pointed with a gunpowder-stained finger. "One of our mortars hit there and knocked the hell out of the enemy."

Ballard looked closer. He could, in fact, see now where some of the loosely built rock wall had been scattered at the top of the ridge. The Chinese already seemed to be spread thin to cover the length of the ridge. They would be spread even thinner at that point.

"All right, let's do it." He looked around for his runner, then sent the kid out to the end of the platoon's position with that message. Sergeant Weber was already hustling away, ready to help push the men up the ridge.

Ballard waved a hand to indicate that his men should follow, and then ran up the slope toward the gap. Bullets pecked at the dirt around him. He leveled his carbine at the defenders, closer now, and made them duck down with a burst.

A soldier jumped to the top of the low wall, holding a handful of stick grenades. He started to cock his arm back to throw one, but Ballard heard a rifle crack off to his right. He looked that way and saw the sergeant lowering his weapon. The Chinese soldier dropped and there was an explosion as the grenade that he'd been holding went off, taking out whatever defenders were in the area.

Helped by the grenade, the fire from the ridge suddenly slackened and the platoon surged forward. The last twenty feet up the face of the ridge required slinging their rifles and digging in with their hands and knees as men below covered the assault team.

But suddenly, Ballard and the others reached the top of the ridge. He crawled over the low stone wall and dropped down into a trench, weapon at the ready, but the Chinese were running away. He shot one in the back for good measure.

All around him, other soldiers began piling into the trenches, spreading out, eliminating any opposition.

He looked back down the slope. Somehow, his men had managed to outpace the rest of the company that was still struggling up the slope.

Ballard shouted orders, but his men already knew what to do. They had spread out along the ridge, attacking the flanks of the remaining Chinese defenders.

The rest of the company surged up the last few feet of the ridge and climbed into the defenses, making short work of any defenders who hadn't already fled.

They heard a few grenades, a handful of shots, and then a ragged cheer.

Sniper Ridge was back in American hands, hopefully for good this time.

CHAPTER TWENTY-SIX

BACK AT HQ, with typewriters clacking all around him at the offices of *Stars & Stripes*, the young journalist settled himself at the desk and flexed his fingers. Don Hardy had just returned from the front and he felt as if he had so much to describe. He wanted to write about the way that the men had attacked the ridge and beaten back the Chinese yet again. He thought about the soldiers who had kept going up that steep slope no matter what, ignoring the gunfire, grenades, and mortars that rained down upon them. Sometimes, the enemy had resorted to hurling rocks.

Finally, there was the sacrifice of those who had not made it off the ridge, but had paid the ultimate sacrifice. They were young and their names were already forgotten, but they had given everything for this fight. Back home in the States, telegrams would be delivered with the awful news.

How could he ever do them justice?

He gulped down half a mug of black coffee to stave off the exhaustion that threatened to fog his mind. Instantly, the caffeine seemed to clear away the cobwebs the way that a stiff breeze suddenly blows the clouds from the sky.

He gazed down at the typewriter keys in the same determined way that a machine gunner gazed down the barrel of his weapon.

And then he began to write. Words flew as his blunt farm boy's fingertips clacked across the keyboard.

He included a few key details about the overall campaign. The assault to recover Sniper Ridge was just one small part of the Battle of Triangle Hill. So far, several hundred Americans and South Koreans had lost their lives there, and who knew how many Chinese—their losses might be in the thousands. Slowly, slowly, the two sides were fighting their way toward a draw. This wasn't like Patton's tanks rushing toward Germany, this was more like the dismal trenches of the Great War that ended in 1918, a slow war of determination and attrition.

As the hands of the clock on the wall spun relentlessly toward deadline, Hardy got the words down on the page.

One by one, as he finished a page, he rolled it out of the typewriter. He set the finished pages to one side, weighting them down with his coffee mug before the breeze from the ceiling fan overhead could whisk them away.

With a typewriter, there wasn't a lot of revising that could be done. He would have to settle for a few hasty pencil marks in the margins.

He would have liked to rewrite parts, but there was the editor, standing over his shoulder. "You done yet?" the editor asked, sounding exasperated.

Feeling a sense of grave ceremony, he squared the edges of the short stack of papers and handed them to the editor, who snatched them away.

Truly feeling exhausted now, he went in search of more coffee.

When he returned, having filled his mug with a thick sludge from the bottom of the coffee pot, the editor waved him over.

"Sir?"

"Good story, kid. Next time, go easy on the melodrama. Remember that there'll be another hill to fight over tomorrow."

* * *

MAJOR WU WAS with the other troops that had withdrawn after the collapse of the defense at Sniper Ridge. The Americans had paid dearly for their victory. By Wu's estimation, the enemy now held approximately one square mile more of territory in the Taebaek Mountain range. Above the 38th Parallel, Wu knew there were more than 46,000 square miles—most of them held by Chinese forces. The American victory was a pebble in a bucket.

Every battle, won or lost, pushed the UN forces closer to reaching an agreement at the negotiation table because the enemy had little stomach for the lives being lost. The memory of the old war in Europe was still too fresh.

Nonetheless, there had been heavy losses on the Chinese side as well.

He was looking down at one of the casualties now.

The body was torn and battered, but recognizable. It was Li Chen, the celebrated sniper.

He had been shot through the heart.

A photographer stood nearby. "Should I take a photograph of the fallen hero, sir?"

"No, no photos yet," Wu said.

Along with the body, Chen's fellow soldiers had carried the story of what had happened. A murderous enemy sniper had somehow gotten behind the lines and surprised Chen. He hadn't so much as gotten off a shot. The infiltrator was described as having a strange symbol painted on his helmet. The soldiers thought it was a flag of some sort, but it was not a United States flag.

"Perhaps the sniper was from one of the other imperialist nations, sir?" one of the soldiers suggested. "England? Australia?"

Wu shook his head. He was familiar with this flag and with this sniper, having encountered them before. "No, it is what the Americans call a Rebel flag." When the soldier looked at him blankly, he explained, "It is a badge of regional identity."

Looking down at the body, Wu searched his heart for some emotion. After all, he and Chen had spent many hours together. But Wu would have been the first to admit that there was a gulf of differences between them. Chen had been a simple peasant soldier, though gifted with the eyes of an eagle. As a political officer, Wu was something more than a simple foot soldier, and far more ambitious.

Wu realized that he did not feel a sense of loss so much as one of disappointment. Chen had failed. Ultimately, this meant that Wu himself had failed. This left a taste like ash in his mouth.

The American sniper who had slipped behind the lines had rattled everyone. It was not so much that he had defeated Chen, although that was something. Worse, someone had shot a general from a great distance just as he arrived to inspect the forces arrayed there. It had never happened before that a general had been killed in such a way. Due to the timing of events, Wu had no doubt that this assassination had been the work of the same sniper who had killed Chen.

He shook his head, turned away from the torn and bloody body.

The soldiers who had borne back Chen's body also presented Wu with the sniper's rifle—or what was left of it, anyway. The barrel was bent; the bolt was missing.

One of the soldiers held out the smashed remains of the telescopic sight.

"This is how we found it, sir."

Wu smacked his hand away, but he was smiling as he did so. "Are you so much of a fool that you would bring me a smashed rifle sight? What use is it? Better to have brought me a rock, or a stick of wood."

Wu's facial expression did not match his harsh words, and the soldiers fell silent and stood at attention, waiting for Wu to dismiss them.

Wu let them wait a while longer. Chen's defeat created many problems, not the least of which was that it would be bad for morale once word got out that an American sniper was responsible. Worse yet for the major would be the fact that he apparently had not picked the right man for the job.

It would be much, much better for him if Chen had not been killed.

Wu thought about that. He was a spinner of tales, was he not?

Wu looked around at the handful of soldiers who had carried back Chen's body and reported to him. His eyes passed over the stupid one who had presented him with the shattered rifle scope. Finally, his glance fell upon a sturdy soldier holding a Chinese-made Hanyang 88 rifle, which was practically an antique.

"You there, come forward."

"Sir?"

"Are you a good shot with that old rifle?"

"Good enough, sir."

"Excellent."

Next, Wu waved the photographer over and explained what he wanted. He ordered the others to dig a hole and bury the dead sniper. Meanwhile, several photographs were taken of the soldier crouched behind a rock, his sturdy rifle pointed at an imaginary enemy. Wu stood slightly behind the photographer and directed him to take photographs in which the soldier's face was turned away, making it hard to identify him.

When they were finished, Major Wu clapped the soldier on the shoulder, smiling merrily all the while. "Congratulations on your many victories today. You have claimed many enemy lives in the battle and made them pay dearly for their hollow victory."

"Sir?"

"You are now Li Chen, the sniper. Report to me in the morning."

Major Wu had come to the powerful realization that the truth would be whatever he said it was. Li Chen had lived. There would always be a Li Chen. If this man fell, another would take his place. He turned away, a happy grin on his face.

* * *

WITH SNIPER RIDGE RECAPTURED, the Chinese were still occupying the next hill, the one nicknamed Jane Russell for its resemblance to a woman's bosoms, and probably the hill beyond that.

Cole was set up on the ridge, deep in a foxhole, his eye to his rifle scope. One might have thought that the victory at Sniper Ridge would have prompted a brief interlude in the overall battle, but that was not the case.

Early that morning before dawn, the Chinese artillery had opened fire to shell the ridge; the US artillery had fired back. Now that it was light, planes patrolled the sky again, attacking behind the enemy lines where the artillery couldn't reach.

Cole was here to shoot anything that moved. Whenever an enemy soldier made the mistake of showing himself, Cole's crosshairs found him.

He spotted what might be an officer moving from trench to trench. Cole tracked him through the sight and as soon as the man paused, his finger caressed the trigger. Across a gulf of no-man's land, the enemy soldier fell. Automatically, Cole worked the bolt and loaded another shell into the chamber. If he felt any emotion at all about having just shot an enemy soldier, it was a sense of satisfaction that he'd been on target.

Behind him, he heard the scuffle of careful movement across the rocks and dirt that formed the network of trenches and foxholes on the ridge. Some had been dug by the Chinese, and some by the American forces, so jumbled now that it was impossible to tell which was which. It was necessary to keep one's head down because the enemy still had its snipers—they just weren't as deadly as Cole.

He was working alone. There should only be Americans up here, but you never knew. The Chinese were still making their infiltrations behind the lines, made even easier by the fact that they'd had plenty of time to get the lay of the land around here. He glanced up long enough to catch a glimpse of the soldier working his way toward him. Satisfied that there wasn't any danger, he got back on the scope.

A few minutes later, the kid crawled into the foxhole. "It's me," he said. "Don't shoot."

"Kid, I heard you comin' from about a mile off," Cole said. "You done made more noise than a herd of buffalo."

"Yeah, well, not everybody is you."

"You can say that again, kid. Why the hell did you crawl all the way out here?"

"I brought you a canteen full of hot coffee. Well, it was hot when I left, anyway."

"That's right good of you," Cole said. The morning was chill and the coffee was only lukewarm and had too much sugar in it, but what he said to the kid after taking a big swig was, "Damn, that's good. Still hot."

The kid smiled. "Also, I brought you a letter. Pomeroy wrote to us."

"Yeah?"

Sitting there in the dirty foxhole, the kid unfolded the clean white sheet of paper and read it aloud to Cole. Pomeroy was doing all right. It seemed that he was getting a Purple Heart.

Not bad for getting drilled through the ear, he wrote.

" 'Drilled through the ear,' " Cole said. "I like that. Ol' New Jersey always had a way with words."

After a while, the kid said, "I ought to start back before it gets dark. What about you?"

"I'm gonna stay a while and see if I can do any good."

"OK, then. Keep your head down."

It was funny to hear the kid tell him that. He could hear the kid slithering through the trenches and ditches for a long ways off. *Definitely a herd of buffalo*, Cole thought. *Maybe even two herds.*

He spotted another enemy soldier moving furtively, running hunched over. It was too far for a running shot. The man jumped down into a hole and disappeared. Cole waited patiently, his scope on the place where he had last seen the runner. Eventually, the man started to crawl out of the hole.

Cole's finger touched the trigger, and the enemy soldier fell back into the hole for good.

A rifle cracked in the distance. Cole heard the whine of a bullet coming in from the enemy's hill. Not too close, but he must have stirred the pot over there. Some new sniper was at work, trying to take Cole's measure.

Cole grinned. The war wasn't over yet, he thought. Not by a long shot.

-The End-

ABOUT THE AUTHOR

David Healey lives in Maryland where he worked as a journalist for more than twenty years. He is a member of the International Thriller Writers and a contributing editor to The Big Thrill magazine. Visit him online at:

www.davidhealeyauthor.com
or
www.facebook.com/david.healey.books

Thank you for reading! If you enjoyed the story, please consider leaving a review on Amazon.com.

Printed in Great Britain
by Amazon